Also published by The New York Review Children's Collection

Uncle
by J. P. Martin
Illustrated by Quentin Blake

J. P. MARTIN

UNCLE
CLEANS UP

illustrated by Quentin Blake

THE NEW YORK REVIEW CHILDREN'S COLLECTION
New York

THIS IS A NEW YORK REVIEW BOOK
PUBLISHED BY THE NEW YORK REVIEW OF BOOKS
435 Hudson Street, New York, NY 10014
www.nyrb.com

First published in Great Britain by Jonathan Cape, Ltd., 1965
Published here by arrangement with
Random House Children's Books, London

Library of Congress Cataloging-in-Publication Data
Martin, J. P. (John Percival)
Uncle cleans up / by J. P. Martin ; illustrated by Quentin Blake.
p. cm. — (New York Review Books children's collection)
Summary: The continuing escapades of Uncle, the unimagin-
ably rich elephant, as he struggles to defend his vast ramshackle
castle against the onslaught of the scruffy Badfort Crowd from the
dingy fortress across the way.
ISBN 978-1-59017-276-6 (alk. paper)
[1. Elephants—Fiction. 2. Kings, queens, rulers, etc.—Fiction. 3.
Castles—Fiction. 4. Animals—Fiction. 5. Humorous stories.] I.
Blake, Quentin, ill. II. Title.
PZ7.M36317Uo 2008
[Fic]—dc22
2007051649

ISBN 978-1-59017-276-6

Cover design by Louise Fili Ltd.

Printed in the United States on acid-free paper.

1 3 5 7 9 10 8 6 4 2

CONTENTS

To
Stella, Grace,
John and Hal

Some of the Characters

Uncle's Followers

The Old Monkey
The One-Armed Badger
Goodman
Butterskin Mute
Cloutman
Gubbins
Cowgill
Noddy Ninety
Oldeboy
Mig
Don Guzman
Whitebeard
Captain Walrus
The Respectable Horses
The King of the Badgers
Wizard Blenkinsop
Will Shudder
Mr Benskin
Joseph Cadcoon
Wisdom Sage
Needler

The Badfort Crowd

Beaver Hateman
Nailrod Hateman (Sen.)
Nailrod Hateman (Jun.)
Filljug Hateman
Sigismund Hateman
Flabskin
Hitmouse
Oily Joe

Hootman
Jellytussle
Abdullah the Clothes-Peg Merchant
The Wooden-Legged Donkey
Wizard Snipehazer
Laurence Goatsby
Professor Gandleweaver
Gasparado
Simon Eggman

Others

Sir Ben Bandit
Mrs Pointer
Miss Jezebel Pointer
Mr Richard Pointer
Mr Friendship Pointer
Mr T. Smiggs Pointer
Tom Fullglass
Mrs Smallweed
Rugbo
Your Syd
Ivan Koff
Len Footganger
Thomas Glot
Walter Meal
Badgers
Wolves
Leopards
Etc., etc.

Hated by Both Sides

Old Whitebeard

UNCLE is an elephant. He's immensely rich, and he's a B.A. He dresses well, generally in a purple dressing-gown, and he often rides about on a traction engine, which he prefers to a car.

He lives in a house called Homeward, which is hard to describe, but try to think of about a hundred skyscrapers all joined together and surrounded by a moat with a drawbridge over it, and you'll get some idea of it.

ONE

Tea on the Lawn

AFTER Uncle's victory over the Badfort crowd he felt he could look forward to a peaceful summer.

"I really think we've dealt with them this time," he said, but the Old Monkey, his faithful friend and helper, was not so sure.

It had been a great victory. Uncle and his supporters had driven off Beaver Hateman and his gang after a fierce fight.

Now it was a time of celebration—of fireworks and banquets and messages of congratulation. Letters, telephone calls and greetings telegrams poured in. And so many visitors came to see Uncle that for a time he behaved with extra politeness and did a good deal of entertaining.

One fine afternoon he asked several important neighbours to tea on the lawn outside his immense castle of Homeward.

"Let's do the thing properly," Uncle said to the Old Monkey. "What about some of those big striped umbrellas? They'd look very festive set up along the edge of the moat."

"Oh yes, sir," agreed the Old Monkey, "and Cheapman has a good stock at a halfpenny each."

Cheapman's Store is in Badgertown. It is a delightful shop where you can get all sorts of splendid things for a halfpenny.

So the tables were set out under the gay umbrellas. The many-coloured towers of Homeward, with switchback railways and chutes strung almost like glittering necklaces between them, looked magnificent in the sunshine. A little distance across the moat lay Badfort, the home of Beaver Hateman, Uncle's enemy. The sight of this huge dingy fortress, always in need of new glass for broken windows, was a constant annoyance to the inhabitants of Homeward. However, the Old Monkey and Cowgill, Uncle's engineer, had placed the umbrellas so that the party would face the massive drawbridge that spanned the blue waters of the moat—a much more pleasant view.

"Pity the King of the Badgers can't come," said Uncle.

The King of the Badgers is one of Uncle's best friends and neighbours, but he was away arranging a loan from a foreign banker.

Unfortunately, Uncle's brother, Rudolf, the big-game hunter and traveller, could not be at the party either. After giving valuable help to Uncle in his great fight with Beaver Hateman and the Bads, he had gone back to his exploration of the Lester-Lester Mountains.

"We'll ask Ivan Koff and Len Footganger," said Uncle.

Ivan Koff comes of a noble Polish family. He has splendid manners, and looks well when he is dressed up, but he *is* rather touchy. For instance, if he sees someone with a slightly larger egg than he has, he thinks nothing of throwing a teapot at that person's head.

Len Footganger appears to know all sorts of important people. He dresses well, but a funny thing about him is that though he wears a well-cut morning coat he wears no shirt with it. Still, this doesn't matter as he spreads his tie over his chest and wears a lot of medals. They are made of rather thin tin, but he explains that he has left his real ones at home. He always carries a great book, *The House of Zillagicci*, which he says is a history of some near relatives.

Uncle also asked a very respectable person, Thomas Glot, who lives in a little hut that juts out over a waterfall.

Several of Uncle's supporters were asked to meet these notabilities.

Don Guzman, who looks after Uncle's oil lake at the base of a distant tower in Homeward, was asked. He says he has a huge estate in Andalusia.

Alonzo S. Whitebeard, who is a friend of Uncle's in spite of being rather miserly, was allowed to come on condition that he combed his beard and put on a clean shirt; he agreed, because there is nothing he likes so much as a free tea.

And, of course, Butterskin Mute, Uncle's gardener, who grows such large cabbages and lettuces, came as well. Uncle had asked him to leave his rake behind and not to wear his smock. Without these things he looked rather uncomfortable as he wears nothing underneath except a pair of maroon-coloured trousers and a frightful singlet with brown marks on it. The fact is that Mute is not much of a person for dress, but the moment he smiles you forget this! In any case the Old Monkey lent him a frogged coat with brass buttons on it, so he looked fairly well.

Altogether they made a very smart group. Uncle's purple dressing-gown, and, of course, an elephant's dressing-gown is very big, added a splendid touch of colour. The Old Monkey makes a good waiter and the tea-party looked like being a great success.

They had thin bread and butter with eggs and jam, and some very small cress sandwiches. Some of the guests found Uncle's egg-shell china difficult to manage, but Uncle had no trouble as he was able to lift cups with a little tip at the end of his trunk. Still, he found the cress sandwiches rather a trial. There seemed to be nothing in them, and an egg was not much use to him either. He doesn't like teaspoons, which is understandable, and in fact he was secretly wishing for one of his solid meals of ham, buckets of cocoa and nets full of cabbages.

Thomas Glot ate cress sandwiches in a dignified way, taking very small bites, and between each bite uttering well-balanced remarks about the weather and the state of the crops.

Footganger also ate very elegantly, but I must say he ate a great deal. An egg was soon gone, and, as for cress sandwiches, his fingers hovered over them like butterflies, and in no time, it seemed, the plate of sandwiches was empty. The Old Monkey kept bringing him more, but he had hardly put down a fresh plateful when there was Footganger languidly looking at the empty plate and lifting to his lips another cup of tea.

Don Guzman did not worry over the unsubstantial provisions because he was narrating a terrific story about his estate in Andalusia, to which he hoped to retire very soon and where, it appeared, he kept no less than ninety boarhounds.

Uncle can't bear long stories of any kind, and he was beginning to feel bored by Don Guzman when the Old Monkey, hurrying up with a fresh plate of sandwiches, whispered in his ear:

"Oh, sir, look across the moat! See who's coming!"

Uncle turned to look towards the dusty unmade road which led to Badfort. The Old Monkey was right. Two shabby carts were making their way towards the moat.

The first cart, pulled by the Wooden-Legged Donkey, held Beaver Hateman, who was wearing a particularly ragged sack suit and a battered silk hat with a flag sticking out of the top. This cart also carried a rickety old table and chairs with some legs missing, and a collection of torn black umbrellas. Hitmouse, a wretched little person who is the chief reporter on the *Badfort News* and who lives in a Nissen hut outside Badfort, was sitting by Hateman. He was bristling, as usual, with skewers, and writing in a hating book. The back of the cart seemed filled with a large jelly of a bluish colour, and this, of course, was Jellytussle, a most spiteful character.

The second cart was driven by Nailrod Hateman, while Sigismund and Filljug Hateman crouched among a number of rusty tea-urns and cardboard boxes of food.

Hootman, a kind of ghost, who spends his time plotting against Uncle, was wafting himself along somewhere between the two carts.

"Take no notice of them," said Uncle. "Don't flatter the miscreants by giving them your attention."

But as the Badfort party set up their tables just across the moat it was impossible to ignore them altogether, especially as Uncle was getting tired of the smallness of his repast, and the Badfort crowd had got together from some source or other quite a solid feast. They had large hams, loaves of bread and buckets of tea, and soon began to eat these things in hideous imitation of the polite party so near to them.

Beaver Hateman took a well-cooked ham between his fingers and thumb, and said in a high-pitched voice as he passed it to Nailrod:

"Have another sandwich, Count!"

"No, thank you, but won't you take one of these little cakes?" replied Nailrod, balancing a whole loaf on a very small egg-cup. "They're so light!"

Hitmouse brought Filljug a plum-cake on an imitation lace mat torn out of newspaper.

"I'm such a small eater," said Filljug in a high squeaky voice. "It always takes about twenty bites for me to eat a macaroon."

Uncle was getting very hot. There was no doubt that the Hateman gang were deliberately insulting him.

Then Beaver Hateman took a whole bucket of tea, and in some mysterious way held it in the crook of his little finger.

"I'm so glad I've got this little attachment on the end of my trunk. It's so handy for holding egg-shell china!" he said in a loud offensive voice.

Still Uncle controlled himself, and went on eating, though with a faint heart, the cress sandwiches that were set before him.

All at once Thomas Glot threw down his cup of egg-shell china, and shouted:

"This is a rotten show! Those chaps over there know how to do a tea much better than you!"

Uncle was surprised and hurt, but he was still more upset when Footganger suddenly yelled:

"I've been here two hours, and hardly had a bite!"

This was most unfair, for they had devoured twenty eggs and and nineteen platefuls of sandwiches, besides emptying six three-tiered cakestands of their contents.

"Besides," Footganger went on, "it's so jolly slow! Look, I'll show you a bit of life and action!"

Footganger rose, and balanced a silver teapot on the end of his toe. Then, with a skilful movement, he jerked it on to his forehead, and dipped his head so that tea began to pour out of the spout into his mouth. It was frightfully hot, but he didn't appear to mind that. Then he began to spin the sugar basin on the heel of his boot.

Thomas Glot could juggle too, for he took a plate of sandwiches and threw them into the air, in such an artful way that they came down in a stream, and he stood underneath and snapped them up as they fell.

Meanwhile Beaver Hateman, made bold by the remarks of the visitors, snatched a large fish that was swimming by in the moat, and threw it at Uncle. It hit him on the side of his head with a slack wet noise.

Uncle flushed, and lashed himself thoughtfully with his trunk. He hesitated to begin again the old weary battle with the Badfort crowd. Yet action seemed almost thrust upon him.

"I am a person of peace and order," he began.

"Shut up!" shouted Beaver Hateman. "We don't want to hear the old bike-thief!"

That decided the matter.

Uncle had been extremely patient, but this allusion to an incident of his University days was too much. Once, in his hurry to get to an examination, he had borrowed a bicycle without permission and, being very heavy, broken it. The Badfort crowd never forget this and never let Uncle forget it either. It irritates Uncle more than anything else.

Uncle noticed that the Old Monkey had propped up one of the table legs with a large stone club. It is not usual to take weapons to a tea-party in your own garden, and Uncle had come quite unprepared. Now, ready to his hand, lay the means of delivering a swift answer to these continued insults.

Uncle stooped, picked up the stone club, and hurled it at Beaver Hateman.

It took him by surprise. The first sign the miscreant had that Uncle was in action again was something like an earthquake in the region of his right ear.

This prompt and vigorous action revived Uncle. He was at once his old autocratic self, and turned his back on the Badfort crowd. He even smiled graciously as he watched Footganger balancing chairs on his nose. Then Thomas Glot carried along a table on his back without spilling a drop of tea or milk. As Glot was on his hands and knees under it, the table seemed to run along the ground and up the steps into the hall of Homeward. It was an amusing sight.

Soon Beaver Hateman pulled himself together again.

"You big bully!" he shouted. "I've done nothing to you, and you've injured me badly—maybe *mortally*!"

This did not seem to be true, for he paused and drank off the contents of a jug of iced soup while he was getting his breath.

"I suppose you don't call throwing a flat-fish at your neighbour during a party an injury?" inquired Uncle in masterful tones.

"No, I don't," said Beaver Hateman. "And let me tell you, that I'm going to attack you soon in a very unusual manner. I've been doing a little quiet inspection while you've been giving parties and I've '*acquired*'—note that word—a copy of your book on the secret passages of Homeward. My friend Hootman has done a bit of nosing around, and we've found passages leading into your old castle that you've never dreamed of! Ha, ha, you'll soon find out what we're up to!"

Uncle ducked, but not quickly enough to avoid a teapot that Beaver Hateman flung at him with a lightning movement. By the time that he had got the fluid out of his eyes, the scoundrels were well on their way to Badfort.

Uncle went into Homeward in a thoroughly bad temper. However, he found in the hall a letter that cheered him up.

It read as follows:

FLINT, FLINT, FLINT, BURROUGHS, FLINT, MACKINTOSH, COATES & STAINER, GOBBLE COURT

Dear Sir,

We beg to inform you that our esteemed client Mr Laurence Goatsby was so impressed by your conduct in dealing with certain bandits that he has decided to make over to you the sum of £1,000,000 (One Million Pounds) to be used for any good purpose you may have in mind.

He wishes, however, to make two small conditions:
  (1) The name of the foundation to be
      The Laurence Goatsby Benefit.
  (2) A small statue of Mr Goatsby, which our client will
      dispatch in advance, to be placed in the hall of your
      residence Homeward.
If you agree to these terms Mr Goatsby will himself in due
course bring you the cash in gold ingots.

Yours faithfully,

FLINT, FLINT, FLINT etc.

Uncle read this letter to the Old Monkey.

"We'll have to think this over," he said. Then he added, "This has not been a bad day after all, but I'm getting a bit tired of these polite tea-parties, so we'll have meals as usual in future."

TWO

A Visit to Whitebeard's

UNCLE was not long in sending a reply to the lawyers, and a few days later he had a telephone message from them. The Old Monkey took the message.

"Mr Goatsby is coming at eleven this morning," he reported to Uncle, "and bringing the statue with him."

Mr Goatsby drove up in a gigantic motor. The statue was wrapped in packing cloth, and firmly fixed on a roof luggage carrier.

Goatsby was a singular-looking man. He had great projecting ears, and such small eyes, hidden behind such thick glasses, that you could hardly see them. After a little refreshment, he began to argue with Uncle as to the place where the statue was to be put.

"It would be best in front of the fireplace," Goatsby said, snappishly.

"I'm not so sure," objected Uncle. "It would be awkward to sit round the fire with a statue in our midst."

"I don't see why!"

But Uncle refused to budge.

Goatsby sulked for a minute or two, then had a fresh idea. He walked over to the main picture in the hall at Homeward, the magnificent oil painting of Uncle opening the dwarfs' drinking fountains.

"That's the place," he said, "right under that old picture."

Uncle very rightly objected to this.

"It would destroy the effect of the picture," he said firmly.

At last they placed it in an alcove, where it was fairly noticeable, though Goatsby was not too pleased. Uncle had to tell him that his million-pound gift, though useful, was by no means indispensable. So in the end Goatsby gave in and drove off saying he would return in a few days with the money in the shape of gold ingots.

It was funny that the moment he was left alone with it Uncle felt that the statue of Goatsby began to get on his nerves. It was so very plain-looking. Even the Old Monkey confessed that he wanted to knock off the hateful projecting marble ears.

Uncle was even beginning to consider sending the statue back and doing without the million pounds, but Whitebeard begged him not to.

"Well," said Uncle, "I'd like to get away from it for a bit, anyhow. I think I'll come and stay with you for a day or so, Whitebeard."

Whitebeard turned very pale.

It is true that he had often invited Uncle to come and stay with him, but he had never dreamed that he might actually come. Whitebeard is such a miser that the very thought of providing a meal for himself makes him shudder, and the thought of providing for Uncle put him into a high fever.

Still he could hardly get out of it. He had been staying with Uncle, off and on, for nearly a year. So he gave a ghastly smile, and said it would be a pleasure, but that, being a poor man, he was afraid that his house would be badly stocked.

"That's a pity," replied Uncle, "for I was thinking of bringing Cloutman, Gubbins, Cowgill and the Old Monkey. Still, I dare say we shall manage, for I remember some months ago giving you three barrels of tinned food. You thanked me warmly, and sent them to your house to be used in case of siege, or if visitors came. Those were your very words. These will be ample for the first day, and by that time you will have had time to look round and order in further supplies."

Every word he spoke was like a poisoned dagger turning in Whitebeard's heart.

"We'll go immediately after breakfast," said Uncle.

"Wouldn't it be better to wait till after lunch – or even till after dinner?" begged Whitebeard.

"No," said Uncle, "we'll start in good time, and then you'll have all the morning to prepare a substantial lunch."

Next morning Whitebeard swallowed twice his usual breakfast as a tonic, and also so as to need less of his own food at lunch-time.

Uncle had, however, got among his morning mail a pamphlet on 'The No-Breakfast Slimming Theory', and decided to try it at once.

"I'll go without breakfast this morning," he said to the Old Monkey, "except for a bucket of cocoa. If I feel a bit faint, I'll make up for it at lunch."

Whitebeard looked up with a sickly smile.

"Old Gleamhound says that going without breakfast is very good for most people, but very bad for elephants," he said.

"Don't worry, I'm only going to try it for one day," said Uncle, reassuringly. "Tomorrow when I'm staying with you I'll have breakfast as usual."

At last they started. Several of them were going on the traction engine which was pulling a tender as well. All the people that Uncle had mentioned went, as well as the Old Monkey's father and the Muncle, though the Muncle didn't travel on the traction engine. He had put on a pair of special electric boots; he switched on the motor and they carried him along. The Muncle is always thinking about boots and shoes, and he has lots of pairs, big travelling ones that run on wheels, some smart lemon-coloured ones, and some that are so highly polished that they look like steel.

Cloutman and Gubbins were rather late and had to start without any breakfast. However, as they told Whitebeard, it would be easy to make up at lunch.

They had quite a safe journey. Badfort was quiet, except that a great fat cat, almost the size of a tiger, was hurled violently out of a window into the moat as the traction engine chugged past.

At last they reached Whitebeard's farm. It's hard to see it at first, for it is surrounded by a very high hedge of sharp thorns. Whitebeard dismounted, and unlocked the gate. The moment they were inside and the gate was shut again, he had to climb speedily back on to the engine, for down the drive came a small herd of lean muscular pigs with sharp tusks, and they made straight for him. The fact is that Whitebeard doesn't feed his pigs, and the result is that they have grown lean and wild and are very fast runners. Also they have developed the habit of fighting in packs like peccaries, and are very dangerous.

"It's asking for trouble keeping them so short," said Uncle. "One day they're going to hurt you, Whitebeard."

"Well," replied Whitebeard, "if there's anything left over from lunch, I may give it them!"

This was not likely to happen, for Whitebeard gathers up fragments of meals in a bag which he hides under his beard and saves them for himself. He eats them in the middle of the night with tremendous relish.

When they got in, they all sat down in a perfectly neat room with a door at the end of it labelled 'Larder'.

Whitebeard told them to be seated. They looked a massive and hungry company sitting there, as Whitebeard went with trembling hands to the larder, unlocked the door, and then gave a shout of surprise.

"Oh, I say," he said, "there's hardly a thing in the cupboard! Someone must have been stealing my supplies!"

Uncle knew perfectly well that this was a lie. It might be all that Whitebeard had in that cupboard, but it was not all his store.

"Scatter, boys," said Uncle, "and search the house for hidden supplies!"

All Uncle's followers are good at finding secret passages and hiding-places, and it was not long before Cloutman gave a joyous cry: "Come here, sir. Just look at that!" A whole wall of the room had moved on rollers, and inside was a really well-fitted grocer's shop, with a counter, scales, a till, shopping baskets and string. On the shelves was one of the best displays of provisions that Uncle had ever seen.

As a matter of fact Whitebeard is so miserly that he can't even bring in food from his own store without pretending to strike a bargain with himself. He pretends there is a shopman there, and offers eightpence for a ninepenny tin of salmon. He then pays the money into the till and feels he has struck a good bargain.

Uncle looked grave. "Whitebeard, you have lied to me. I'm sorry to say it of a personal friend, and I would take a stronger action, if I did not remember how well you served me in a supreme hour of peril by wheeling up that truck-load of stone clubs. You will now serve us with your costliest and choicest provisions, and those in unlimited quantities!"

Whitebeard was horror-struck.

"Oh no, sir!" he gasped. "Not *choicest*! Not most *costly*!" Then, in a kind of shriek: "Not UNLIMITED QUANTITIES!!"

However Uncle thought Whitebeard needed a lesson, so they all sat down to a mighty feast.

"That's my ninth tin of preserved ginger," said Cloutman to Gubbins, "and really, I think it tastes better than the first!"

The room they were sitting in looked out on the garden where there was a statue of Whitebeard.

"Strange," said Uncle, "I don't remember seeing that statue before, Whitebeard."

"I've never seen it myself," said Whitebeard. At that moment the pack of lean angry pigs came round the corner and made a rush at the statue which they thought was Whitebeard himself. As the pigs rushed up, the figure was quickly drawn back on a plank into a recess in the wall. Two of the pigs rushed after it, and the flap was then quickly closed.

"I come here," said Uncle, rather crossly, "to get away from one statue, and here is another. I seem haunted by statues!"

The Old Monkey ran upstairs to look out of a window, and came back with the explanation of the mystery.

"Beaver Hateman and a sort of shadowy chap are loading those two pigs into a cart pulled by the Wooden-Legged Donkey," he said.

"Well," said Uncle, striking his trunk on the table with a resounding blow, "that's clever! I can see that the ghost Hootman is behind this. It's far too smart for Beaver Hateman. There'll be roast pork in Badfort tonight!"

As he spoke, they heard a loud shriek, and an old man came sprinting round the house pursued by the rest of the wild pigs.

"That's your father, Whitebeard," said Uncle.

"Oh dear," said Whitebeard, "I didn't know he was coming."

Whitebeard's father is a detestable man. His son appears almost lovable by his side. He dresses in would-be fashionable clothes, and has a laugh which makes every living creature shrink away. But at the moment he was not laughing at all; he was screaming, and I may say that his scream is far better than his laugh.

As he came round for the second time, he saw Whitebeard in the window. "Alonzo!" he called in a piercing voice. "My son! My son!"

But a great black boar was snapping at his heels, so he tore off again.

As he came round for the fourth time, he was slowing down. "This can only end one way," said Uncle, gravely.

But he was wrong, for Whitebeard's father suddenly stopped, drew himself to his full height, and gave vent to a laugh so sickening that every pig paused. Then he laughed again. So abominable was his merriment that the swine seemed to lose strength.

With an odious chuckle he stooped forward and said:

"The pigs, the dear little pigs, how I love the DEAR LITTLE PIGS!!"

And he tried to put his hand on the head of a pink sow that had been foremost in the chase, but he laughed again so foully that the pigs began to shrink away into the bushes. Also a number of plants and shrubs near by began to droop and wilt.

Laughing hideously, Whitebeard's father then walked towards the house.

Whitebeard turned to Uncle, looking worried.

"This has been a day of great strain to me, sir," he said, "and if my father is allowed to come in I feel that I shall be seriously ill!"

Others felt the same, and Uncle took up a seven-pound tin of corned beef and threw it haughtily at the detestable man's feet.

"Now, be off!" he said.

And to everybody's surprise and relief Whitebeard's father went.

THREE

Uncle's Treasury

W HEN Uncle came back from Whitebeard's, he settled down to his usual breakfast routine.

The Old Monkey came cheerfully in with two buckets of cocoa and a great basket of breadfruit and bananas. But Uncle, instead of reading the paper, was looking gloomily at the statue of Goatsby.

"I don't like the way its ears stick out," he said.

"No, sir, nor do I," agreed the Old Monkey. "And it's got such a sneering expression. I don't feel at home with it in the room."

"I suppose I'll have to get used to it," said Uncle, turning his back on the statue. "The gold ingots will be coming this afternoon."

"Where will you be putting them, sir?"

"In my treasury. We'll all go together to deposit it."

"Oh good, I've never been to the treasury," said the Old Monkey, in high spirits once again.

Uncle collected a strong company together to move the gold ingots. He sent for Cloutman and Gubbins and Captain Walrus, while Noddy Ninety was also told to come, for he's a shrewd old chap, and good at watching against treachery. Ninety, although very old, likes to dress up as a schoolboy and go to Dr Lyre's school in Lion Tower. He knows the work so well by now that he starts in the bottom form on Monday and is in the top form by Friday afternoon. He is also very good at cricket. He works on the trains of Homeward during the holidays.

The gold ingots arrived in ten large wagons. The gold was in the form of polished bricks and bars, and looked very handsome shining in the sun.

Uncle had told Cowgill to be prepared for the transport of heavy materials, and he was ready with a number of motor-lorries.

Uncle's henchmen made an imposing sight drawn up in the hall, and Goatsby seemed very much impressed by the massive figures of Cloutman and Gubbins and the venerable, but tough form of Noddy Ninety.

"Didn't know you had all these chaps working for you!" he said. "Well, it will take the whole lot of them to shift this stuff. Do you know that it takes two strong men all their time to lift one of the smallest of these ingots?"

Uncle motioned to Gubbins, and Gubbins, without the slightest effort, picked up two of the largest ingots and flung them into a truck.

Goatsby was amazed. "This is a valuable helper of yours!" he said, in rather a jealous voice.

"Oh, the others are just as good in their way," replied Uncle. "Cloutman, for instance, can strike down a lion with one blow!"

"Let's get the stuff in," said Goatsby, irritably. "I suppose you have a suitable place to put it?"

"Yes," replied Uncle, in a grave, dignified voice, "my treasury."

He took from his pocket a small key, and went into a room adjoining the hall. Then everybody heard a loud, piercing noise rather like a buzz-saw and Uncle motioned them to approach. What they saw surprised them.

The whole floor of the room had risen up to the ceiling. Where the floor had been, a long smooth passage of brilliantly lighted steel sloped gently downwards.

"Drive the lorries in carefully," said Uncle, "and then everybody can sit on them and we'll start. Are you all here?"

They were all there except Alonzo S. Whitebeard, who was discovered in a fainting condition. The sight of so much gold had made him positively ill. However, Uncle happened to have in his pocket a packet of Gleamhound's Faintness Producer for

Burglars. On it were the words: 'Guaranteed to protect the timid
housewife. Simply place a couple on your adversary's tongue, and
he falls into a deep coma.' As Gleamhound's remedies work
backwards he slipped two into Whitebeard's mouth and he revived,
and stretched himself admiringly by the side of a large ingot.

The lorries glided down the sloping passage and after a long
journey drew up at a huge barrier of massive steel.

Uncle's treasury is guarded by a very good sentry called Oldeboy. As the lorries stopped they saw him looking out from his
sentry-box which had a flame-thrower fixed on the top of it.
Oldeboy is only about sixteen, but he is always pretending to be
old. He admires Noddy Ninety so much that he copies him in
every way possible, even wearing an artificial beard and large
spectacles. He is very sharp-witted and makes a first-rate sentry.

"Stand, every one of you, and then come up to the light!" he
said and switched on a powerful electric lamp.

"Have I got to do this?" asked Goatsby crossly.

"Let's have a look at you, one by one, or I'll turn the flame-
thrower on you!" was Oldeboy's answer to that.

When he had examined them he turned to Uncle.

"Right, you can unlock the gate, sir. I have to be careful, you
know. Only last week a fellow arrived disguised as Whitebeard.
He was all beard and whiskers. I wasn't satisfied so gave him a
taste of the flame-thrower. That scorched his whiskers off, and
who do you think it was?"

"I know—Beaver Hateman," said Uncle. "That man's foul
trail is everywhere!"

"He went off down the passage like a firework, sir."

"You've done finely, Oldeboy, finely!" said Uncle.

"Need I go to Dr Lyre's school any more, sir?" asked Oldeboy.
"It makes me feel too young."

"You stay while you can! It's a fine school!" shouted Ninety.

"You can guard my treasury for the time being, but your studies must continue," said Uncle. "In the meantime here is a little present I have been keeping for you."

He handed Oldeboy a bottle labelled 'Gleamhound's Youth and Beauty Foam. Turns a withered, wrinkled hag into a peach-complexioned sylph in a few minutes. Simply rub in.'

"Oh, sir," said Oldeboy, "I want to look very old!"

"Listen to him," said Ninety in disgust. "What I'd give to look as well as he does in a school cap!"

"Don't you know that Gleamhound's medicines work backwards? You'll find this effective. Try it."

Oldeboy rubbed in the lotion and in a moment had the wrinkled face of an old man; his very eyes looked dim and his face seemed to fall in.

"And," said Uncle, "in case your mother doesn't like your looks, here is a little tin of Gleamhound's Old Man Ointment."

"I thought we were coming to a treasury, not a beauty parlour," said Goatsby.

Uncle felt annoyed at this, but he said nothing, only giving the signal for the lorries to move on. At last they reached the treasury, passing through nine steel doors—each of which had to be unlocked—to get there.

Uncle's treasury resembles a vast cave lined with steel. Valuables are piled everywhere in majestic confusion. The vast room is about half full, but Uncle directed the lorries to be pushed into an open space in front of a mighty pile of gold. Then he directed Cloutman to unload the gold bars.

As a matter of fact Goatsby's million pounds worth of gold didn't seem to make much difference. "You have to look twice to see if it's there, don't you?" said Uncle.

This seemed to be too much for Goatsby, who turned away from the pile of gold and said:

"Well, let's get back."

As a matter of fact Uncle wanted to get home by six o'clock as he was expecting a very special parcel by the second post, so he gave the signal to return.

The journey to the treasury had made Uncle forget Goatsby's statue, but as soon as he got back to the hall of Homeward its ugliness made him shudder. The marble ears seemed to stick out even further, and it was depressing to think that having accepted the gold ingots he now had this hateful object in his living-room for ever.

"Oh, look at my statue!" cried Goatsby. "It's not very well dusted, is it?"

"You had better remove it if you don't like the way it is kept," said Uncle, breathing heavily.

"Oh no, your room would look so empty and drab without it! I'm sure you won't mind me coming every week and bringing a feather duster!"

This insult to the Old Monkey's housekeeping was too much for Uncle. "Look," he said, "to tell you the truth I'm tired of your statue, Goatsby. You can take it away."

The Old Monkey jumped for joy.

"What about the gold ingots?" said Goatsby, with an odious smile. "No statue, no ingots."

Uncle went to his desk and took out his cheque-book.

"I will pay you for the ingots and that will finish the matter! That is unless you would like me to take the gold out of the treasury again."

"Oh, we can't go through all that again!" said Goatsby. "I'll take the cheque."

"You'll have to cash it here," said Uncle. "There's no bank in the country that could meet such a sum. And I reserve the right to pay in cash or goods. I'll think the matter over. You can present the cheque tomorrow. But you can remove your statue now. It may be a good likeness, but it takes away my appetite and spoils my breakfast."

Goatsby said nothing, but took the cheque. Then he did a very strange thing. He began to dance in front of his statue. They all watched him while he bowed and scraped and whirled for a long time.

After he had gone with the statue Uncle sighed:
"Well, that's a relief. I must say. I'm much puzzled though by
Goatsby's conduct. That dance, what did you make of it?"
"I don't know I'm sure, sir," said the Old Monkey. "It was as
though he had won a victory, but how could he have done?"
"Very mysterious," said Uncle.
A few minutes later a telegram arrived from Badfort.

DEAR OLD CLEVER-BOOTS, GOATSBY JUST ARRIVED.
THE GOLD HE BROUGHT YOU IS GILT LEAD. TOMORROW
WE CASH CHEQUE AND HOLD FESTIVAL BANQUET.

BEAVER HATEMAN

Uncle turned pale as he read this. He felt very depressed and
so did the Old Monkey.
As for Whitebeard, despite the medicine he had recently taken,
he was lying on the floor in a state of collapse.
"A cheque for a million!" he kept muttering.
"I'll tell you what, sir," said the Old Monkey. "I'll give you all
my savings to help you out."
This was very generous of the Old Monkey, for he had got
together, in one way or another, a hundred pounds. He does
Uncle's accounts, but even so he doesn't really understand the
meaning of a million pounds.
"No," said Uncle. "Thank you all the same. I shan't need that,
but I shan't forget the offer."
Incredible as it may seem, there did come a time when Uncle
actually needed the Old Monkey's money, and very badly, in a
terrible emergency.
"I must honour my own cheque," said Uncle, "but I've got to
save my face somehow; the question is how!"

"We must think of something!" said the Old Monkey. "We can't let Goatsby win over this."

"I've got it," said Uncle suddenly slapping down his trunk, "I'll ring up Wizard Blenkinsop and see if he can show me a way out."

"Oh, splendid, sir," said the Old Monkey.

Uncle went to the telephone and asked for Wizard Glen 88.

Blenkinsop replied at once, and Uncle explained the matter. The Wizard said that the best way was for them to come and see him and meanwhile he would think out a plan.

They decided to set out that very night, for Uncle felt he couldn't sleep till something was settled.

They left Whitebeard weeping and swallowing pie and sandwiches in order to recover his strength.

FOUR

They Visit Wizard Blenkinsop

IT IS not very far to the Glen. They did not take the traction engine as the road there is very rough. It was coming on wet, so they wore mackintoshes. Uncle's mackintosh is just a big tarpaulin that fits him like a haystack, but the Old Monkey has rather a smart, bright yellow one with a belt. It doesn't suit him very well. It has such a huge collar that it makes his face look too small, and, as he was wearing an enormous yellow sou'wester as well, he seemed all mackintosh.

But they shuffled along. Uncle had some clips inside his mackintosh to hold one or two stone clubs; otherwise they didn't take much.

It seems easy enough to get to the Glen, yet when you try it's hard. You go by railway right through the castle, and get out at a little station called Cake Loop. Right in front of you is a signpost: TO WIZARD GLEN.

The road is good for the first few yards. Then it becomes very muddy, then very slippery, then full of round pebbles that turn under your feet. Then like jelly. They could see the Glen right in front, yet it took more than an hour to get there, and all the time it kept getting wetter and wetter. The rain was coming down like a river as they reached the entrance.

A downcast-looking man was sitting by a brazier. He was wearing three mackintoshes and an overcoat. He had a great drum of carbide by him. He kept casting lumps into the brazier, and they burnt in the rain. The more the rain came down, the bigger the flame, but it gave out a most atrocious smell.

"Who's that?" he shouted in a dismal voice as Uncle came up. "I can't see you."

With these words he emptied half a drum of carbide into a puddle and lit it with a match. A great sickly-yellow flame sprang up and the smell became, if possible, worse.

"Oh, it's Uncle," he said at last. "I hardly knew you in that tarpaulin. And is that the Old Monkey? He looks just like a walking mackintosh. Well, push on, Blenkinsop's expecting you, but you must be careful. It's very wet further on!"

They passed him. It grew darker, and much wetter, and soon they reached a bend in the Glen where the thunder roared and the lightning flashed all the time. The ground was a foot deep in water and blue with electric flashes.

But all at once this changed, and they found themselves out of the storm. They looked back and saw behind them what looked like a wall of water blue with flares and roaring with explosions.

Right in front of them was a black, square house with I. BLENKINSOP on the roof in letters of flame. By the side of the door was a brass plate which read:

I. BLENKINSOP—WIZARD
Branch Office at Sable Gulf

They rang the bell, and a sandy-haired boy came to the door.

"You want to see Mr Blenkinsop? Well, he's just having his supper, but come into the office and I'll ask him."

The office was a very ordinary place, except that some of the chairs kept getting bigger and then smaller, and a great white cat was weighing parcels in a corner.

The cat seemed to take a fancy to the Old Monkey, and, seeing one of the parcels had come undone, took a piece of dried fish out of it and pushed it along the desk to him with a ruler.

"Put that fish back!" said a piercing voice.

The cat hastily began to wrap up the parcel again, but he soon stopped to write a hasty note to the Old Monkey: 'He can see through walls!'

The Old Monkey shuddered.

Just then the young man came back and said:

"He says you can come in now."

When they entered Blenkinsop's office they found him sitting at a roll-top desk. He was a little man with cloudy eyes and wore old-fashioned breeches and stockings. He also took snuff, but he was quite up-to-date in his brand; for a tin of Gleamhound's Paralysing Snuff (Anti-Burglar) stood on the table, and the Old Monkey could read on the label:

'Simply throw one pinch into a burglar's face. He immediately becomes helpless for hours.'

Blenkinsop took a refreshing pinch as they came in, and tossed his supper dishes into the mouth of a four-foot-high rubber frog that stood by his desk. The mouth immediately closed, and a swishing, washing-up sound followed.

"Now I am ready," said Blenkinsop, "and as this is a regular consultation my charge is two guineas."

Uncle took out the money and laid it on the table. "Thank you," said Blenkinsop. "Now I will give you my opinion. This is a serious matter, and I have thought it out myself. The smaller difficulties I usually refer to my oracle machine!"

He pointed to a machine in the form of an iron statue.

"I use this a good deal," said Blenkinsop. "It's only five shillings for an opinion. You write the question on a card, put it into the statue's hand, turn a handle at the back, and a typed answer comes out of the little door in front. Here are some ready for the post.

Uncle took one of the cards, and read:

Question:
>I cannot keep my eggs from going bad. Have tried water-glass, but at the end of ten years they are slightly musty. What shall I do?

Answer: Place them in a wooden box smeared with lime juice. They will be fresh at the end of fifty years, but do not open them before that time or they may go stale suddenly.

Then another:

Question: How can I be cured of baldness?

Answer: Smear the head with water-resisting glue; and then sprinkle with chopped badger hair.

"Now I think," said Blenkinsop, "that each of those answers is a good five bob's worth! By the way, they should be posted. Where's Goodman the cat? And my little instrument for seeing through walls? Oh, I say, the idle rotter! He's watching a rat-hole!"

He gave a loud shout:

"Goodman!"

Goodman at once left the rat-hole and came into the office.

"How often have I told you: no mouse- or rat-catching during office hours!" said Blenkinsop.

"It was a huge rat," said Goodman sulkily. "He was after the office paste!"

"That's no excuse. You know you only do it for pleasure. Here, take these cards and post them, and be quick about it!"

The cat seemed unwilling to go.

"The post is right down the Glen," he said, "and I shall get wet! And, besides, I'm working overtime for nothing! I reckon to stop at six. And I haven't had that rise in wages. Three saucers a day is rotten pay. Rotten!"

"You shut up," replied Blenkinsop, "or I'll put a spell on you. Now be off to the post!"

"Can I lend him my mackintosh, Mr Blenkinsop?" asked the Old Monkey.

"If you want to," said Blenkinsop, rather crossly.

They had great trouble in getting the mackintosh on to Goodman. It was far too big, and kept slipping. At last they bundled it on, and the cat, looking like a great waterproof parcel, started slowly down the Glen.

"Idle, slovenly, sleepy rascal!" said Blenkinsop.

Uncle said nothing, but he thought that the wizard was rather too hard on his employee, and this view was confirmed now that the cat had gone, because there was a joyful squeak, and the office became filled with great rats.

"Drive them out!" shouted Blenkinsop, furiously.

He ran in himself, striking right and left, but was not in time to prevent a grey-whiskered fellow from dragging a small parcel down his hole. Meanwhile the young man in the office, whose name was Walter Meal, was not lifting a finger to help. He was pretending to add up a column of figures, and had got them all wrong, as Uncle saw. He took no notice of the rat hunt.

They settled down after a while, and then Blenkinsop gave Uncle his opinion about Goatsby and the million pounds. It was this:

"Pay Goatsby, but pay him in pig iron and have it melted into a solid immovable mass in front of Badfort!"

Uncle was much struck by this idea. He would save his face by honouring his cheque, and Beaver Hateman and his gang would be scarcely any better off. A solid mass of iron could cost nearly as much to cut up as it was worth.

"What a brilliant idea!" he said. He was so pleased with it that he gave the wizard a big five-pound piece as well as the regular fee.

They were now ready to return home, but the Old Monkey had no mackintosh, so they had to wait.

At last they saw Goodman, the cat, coming slowly up the path. He looked a miserable object. His front paws were in mackintosh sleeves that dragged on the ground, but he hobbled on steadily.

"Did you post them?" said Blenkinsop.

"Well, sir, the pillar-box was under water, but there was an otter there who seemed a decent chap. He dived down to put them in."

"You unspeakable ass!" shouted Blenkinsop. "They'll all be spoiled! Look here, Goodman, you can clear out, and I'll get another cat."

The Old Monkey whispered to Uncle. He had often wished they had a cat, and he had taken a real liking to Goodman.

Uncle nodded. They were getting over-run with mice at Homeward, and Goodman would make a nice companion for the Old Monkey. Besides, he himself had taken rather a fancy to the strange creature.

So it was settled. Goodman had no mackintosh, but Uncle said that he could walk along inside his tarpaulin.

The wizard was not altogether pleased, but he was always changing his cats and a miserable little tabby had been round asking for work at low wages—two saucers a day. So perhaps he could try it for a time.

As for the cat Goodman, he was absolutely delighted, for the Old Monkey whispered to him that he'd get unlimited milk and fish, and that his boss was very kind to animals.

I must say that Goodman is a very interesting creature. He's much larger than most cats, and very playful, though he looks grave and thoughtful. He told the Old Monkey that he thought he could help Uncle a lot because he could walk very quietly and find out things.

They got back rather late, and Uncle gave Goodman a can of milk that fairly took his breath away—about a gallon—and then told him that he could sleep by the hall fire, but he was to sleep very lightly, and keep listening. He would be allowed to doze a good deal during the day because Uncle wouldn't have so much for him to do except wrapping up parcels and stamping letters. Goodman loves stamping letters. He licks the stamps as if he enjoyed the taste of the gum, and puts them all on straight.

"Right you are, sir!" replied the cat. "And I'll tell you this. If a mouse or a rat so much as shows his nose in this hall, I pity him. He won't do it twice. The whole bally crew will get the wind up. Let them show their noses, only their *noses*, at the hole, and they'll think it's the end of the world! There were a hundred great rats that banded themselves together once to try to do me in. They came in platoons down a place called Cheesy Hole. Do you think I cared? I did 'em in, I tell you, I did 'em in!"

"Don't talk so much," said Uncle, but he was secretly smiling a little.

"Right you are, sir," said Goodman cheerfully. "I'll have another saucer of milk. Three saucers a day, the wizard gave me, and nothing extra for overtime—carrying letters and parcels, *and* in my spare time—and I was also supposed to catch fish for Mr Blenkinsop!"

At last they turned in. Uncle slept well, for he thought he could see a way through the mesh of difficulties that surrounded him.

FIVE

The Big Casting

WHEN Uncle came down the next morning the first thing he saw was the cat Goodman chasing a piece of brown paper round the room. The moment he saw Uncle, he straightened up and began to sort the letters. When Uncle sat down to breakfast, he found on his plate two fresh trout. Goodman had been out exploring and had caught them for him.

Goodman behaved very well at breakfast. He had a seat next to the Old Monkey, and he drank his milk like a gentleman. His only lapse from good manners was when Uncle gave him one of the fish. Then he rushed from his chair spinning the trout along the ground and pouncing on it. But Uncle excused that because Goodman was not used to sitting at the table, but usually drank from a saucer on the floor and looked for rats at the same time.

He only had one really bad habit. He loved to read the morning paper, and on this first morning he jumped on Uncle's chair and tried to look over his shoulder. Uncle couldn't stick that. He decided to order Goodman a paper of his own.

In any case, Uncle had little time to look at any paper. He had to push on with preparations for getting the million pounds' worth of iron melted down in front of Badfort. He rang up Cowgill, and Cowgill thought it would be a big job, but said he believed he could manage it.

The difficulty was getting the iron there.

At last Uncle thought of a plan. There are a million dwarfs who are his tenants, and he decided to employ the lot for one day as carriers, and to let them off a week's rent besides giving them a free feed of fish and rice.

That left Cowgill free to manage his hundreds of portable furnaces for the smelting. These arrangements took some time, but at about ten o'clock they were ready, and Uncle put on a specially rich gown of purple, and waited contentedly in the warm sunshine.

Soon there was a great rattling and clanging at Badfort. They had erected Goatsby's statue just outside the front door, and crowds of Beaver Hateman's friends were filing past it, singing and laughing.

Then they formed a procession and set out gaily to cash Uncle's cheque for one million pounds.

In front was a cart drawn by the Wooden-Legged Donkey and the lean goat, Toothie, and sitting in the cart were Beaver Hateman in a new red sack suit, Nailrod, Sigismund Hateman, old Nailrod, Flabskin, and Oily Joe. They filled the cart to overflowing; in fact, Oily Joe and Flabskin sat on the ledge at the back and were always falling off.

Beaver Hateman was blowing a trumpet and rattling a great money-box.

By the side of the procession walked that odious man, Alonzo S. Whitebeard's father. He was playing very badly on an accordion, 'See The Conquering Hero Comes'.

At last they reached the moat bridge, and Beaver Hateman got down. He pulled the cheque out of his pocket and said in a menacing voice:

"Well, Uncle, we've come for the million pounds. This is your cheque, isn't it?"

Uncle smiled.

"It is," he said.

"I suppose you're going to try to get off paying?"

"You'll be paid all right, but remember that you can be paid in either goods or money, as I wish," Uncle replied.

"Stop talking. Cash it and be quick about it!" said Beaver Hateman.

Uncle answered this rudeness with one calm and impressive sentence:

"I've decided to pay you the whole sum in the form of pig iron which will be melted down in a great mass in front of your house this afternoon."

Beaver Hateman was furious.

"I don't want iron, you oily old shark!" he shouted.

"Well, that's all you'll get," said Uncle with a smile of quiet triumph.

Beaver Hateman now tried to put the cheque back in his pocket, but he had forgotten the length of Uncle's trunk. In a moment Uncle had seized it and torn it up.

"Now," he said, "push off! ... Oldeboy, have you got that flame-thrower ready?"

"Yes, sir," exclaimed that ready youth, emerging from a clump of bushes with what looked like the nozzle from a fire engine in his hand.

"Well, turn it on when I've counted ten!"

But before he had, the Hateman crowd were walking sulkily back to Badfort. They have a wholesome dread of Oldeboy's flame-thrower.

Whitebeard's father, however, did not go with them. With a ghastly smile he came up and offered his services to Uncle.

"Can I do anything for you, sir?" he asked. "You heard me playing 'The Conquering Hero' for you."

"You were playing it for Beaver Hateman," shouted Uncle.

The sight of Whitebeard's father is nearly enough to make Uncle lose his temper. Now this flattery sickened him. Turning on the lying shifty old scoundrel in righteous indignation, he took a quick run and fairly kicked him up!

It was a magnificent kick. The body of the old hypocrite went up, up, up, in the sunlight, looking far more attractive than it had ever done before, and then came down, down, down, on

the hideous statue of Goatsby that disfigured the front of Badfort. That monstrosity with its hateful projecting ears was knocked to bits.

"Well," said Uncle, "perhaps that was a shade violent, but I just had to do it, and I will say this—a better kick I never made."

After a light lunch, the great removal began. Uncle's plan was to make several journeys, and from the distance the dwarfs looked just like a swarm of ants carrying sticks and leaves. By six o'clock the whole million pounds' worth had been taken across, and then the little men sat down to devour their meal of fish and rice. You could hear their jaws making a faint rustling sound like leaves stirring in the wind.

Then Cowgill's work began. He had gathered together, during the day, a hundred portable blast furnaces. They were wheeled into a semi-circle in front of Badfort. As night came on, the sight was magnificent. From the hundred flaming furnaces melted iron was pouring in streams. They cast the great mass of iron in a hollow place, and it took two or three days to melt it all. At last it was done, the furnaces were wheeled off, and in front of Badfort was a low dull-red mound of solid iron. It cooled down into an almost unbreakable mass.

Beaver did his best to sell it, but it took too much carting, and very few people wanted it.

The Wooden-Legged Donkey pulled over a few loads to Cheapman's, but he soon rebelled at the hard work. Even Beaver Hateman's great offer: 'A ton of iron for a single ham—fetch it yourself' met with no response. Finally he had to admit that the stuff was no good to him.

But he sent a threatening letter to Uncle:

To Uncle, the old crab of Humbug Lodge. Hootman is making a catapult and the whole of your iron will be returned to you in ton pieces. I hope they hit you and crush you flat!

Uncle took no notice of this except to laugh, but he felt more serious when he saw the machine they set up to throw over the pieces of iron. That doubtful character, Abdullah the Clothes-Peg Merchant, was helping Hootman to construct it. There was an immense spring in it which was coiled down by the aid of hundreds of captive badgers.

Uncle could only hope that, like so many of the Badfort schemes, it would not work.

Unfortunately it did work, at least once, for Uncle had gone to the front door of Homeward to welcome the King of the

Badgers when a great lump of iron came zooming through the air and hit the outside dining-table, burying it deep in the ground.

"Oh, sir," cried the Old Monkey, "what an escape!"

"Don't worry," said Uncle, "the labour of breaking off a piece that size must be almost unbearable. They won't do it often."

On the whole, in spite of the catapult, Uncle was very pleased with the iron scheme, and the King of the Badgers was so full of admiration for the way Cowgill had managed the big casting that he came on a special visit to see Cowgill's works.

The King of the Badgers often comes to see Uncle and is very friendly, but it's a pity that he often seems to be hard up. He never buys at Cheapman's for some reason, and such a lot of his subjects are taken into captivity by Hateman that he is always having to ransom them, and this keeps his kingdom rather poor.

Uncle took him with great pleasure to see Cowgill's works, which are part of Homeward. It is a very interesting place as there are all sorts of workers there including a lot of birds. Crows, especially, are very good at screwing on nuts in awkward places. They fly up with the nut, and then, grasping it with their beaks, they fly round and round in circles, and they get it on splendidly.

Cowgill had got all his portable furnaces stowed away, and everything in such good order, that the King bestowed on him one of his highest honours, the Order of the Golden Goat.

With this on his coat, Cowgill felt six inches taller. Uncle also gave him seventy cases of mixed fruit and twelve hundredweight of choice lard, besides a silver tripe bowl, so he felt very happy indeed.

SIX

They Visit the Fish-Frying Academy

FOR a long time Uncle had intended to visit the Fish-Frying Academy. You may remember that on the roof of a great lonely tower he had noticed a big square door battened down, with the words 'Fish-Frying Academy – Goods Entrance' on it. He was a little doubtful about going so far from Homeward as he was pretty certain that Beaver Hateman was planning a tremendous return blow, but they all felt that they wanted a change so he decided to go. He got Captain Walrus to come down and watch the door of Homeward, with the help of Cloutman, Gubbins and Alonzo S. Whitebeard. Captain Walrus was quite pleased. He brought down a great box of marlinespikes and belaying-pins.

"Now," he said, "let the swabs come, and they'll regret it for the rest of their days!"

Uncle decided to take Cowgill this time, as another little reward for his splendid engineering. Also Uncle had heard that it was very hard to get into the Fish-Frying Academy, so they might need to break open that great door, and then Cowgill and his tools would be invaluable.

Also, of course, they took the cat Goodman, and I really believe that he would have done something desperate if he had been left behind. Goodman has a strong turn for adventure and reads a lot of detective stories. Sometimes he lies on the floor in the library gently turning the leaves with his paws and purring loudly at exciting places. When he gets to a very thrilling part, he mews, and sometimes he leaves the book and rushes round the room.

Of course, the One-Armed Badger went. There is nothing he likes better than going on an expedition with Uncle and loading himself to the ground with things that might be wanted. Today he had outdone himself by devising a great pack that so covered

him that you could scarcely see him at all. He looked like a great bale of goods shuffling along. Meat-juice, lint, bandages, cocoa, hams, mince-pies, bottles of milk, preserved fruits, clean socks, telescopes, compasses, axes—there was nothing that he had forgotten.

Cowgill brandished a great four-foot spanner.

"If we do meet any doubtful customers, sir, this will be as good as a stone club any day."

Uncle rather doubted this. He has such a liking for stone clubs that he feels uncomfortable without one when he is going on a journey. All the same, the spanner would be a good stand-by.

He had found out, after some trouble, the best way to the Fish-Frying Academy. You walk along the outside of Homeward until you come to a little room called 'waiting-room'. Then you go in, and simply wait. There's no way out of this room, except through the door by which you came in, but if you wait for a time the whole room begins to move and takes you with it.

On the wall is a card with this message:

Passengers to the Fish-Frying Academy
must be content to wait their turn.

There are always more visitors
than we can accommodate.

Keep quiet, do not cough or sneeze, or *sing*.

Passengers requiring lunch can telephone Hungry 87659.

Passengers can play games if quiet,
but Tiddlywinks, Noughts-and-Crosses, and Halma
are strictly forbidden.

Slogan for today: 'Patience in the waiting-room
means joy in the Fish-Frying Academy.'

Uncle read this notice through, yawned, and sat down on the one decent chair in the place.

"We might as well have a spot of lunch," he said.

They were all agreeable to this, and the One-Armed Badger soon had a splendid repast ready. When it was finished, Uncle said:

"Well, I vote we have a game. If I had Tiddlywinks with me I should play. I'm the master of this castle!" He turned to the One-Armed Badger. "Next time you come this way, bring a set of Tiddlywinks with you."

They felt a bit sorry for the One-Armed Badger; he thought he had brought everything. He offered to go and fetch a set.

"No!" said Uncle. "You'll get left. It doesn't really matter." And he gave the One-Armed Badger a threepenny piece as consolation.

"But I'll tell you what," said Uncle, as another hour dragged by, "I think we might manage a game of spigots. The room is rather small, but I fancy we could do it. There are half a dozen of those round Dutch cheeses and six cake boxes."

Just as he said this someone shouted: "Hold tight!" And they felt the room move.

The next instant they felt a jar, and the same voice shouted: "This way out!"

To their surprise one of the sides of the room had vanished and they were looking down a long tunnel like those in the Underground. They walked along till they came to two branching passages, one labelled 'To The Academy' and the other 'To The Sinking Parade'.

"I wonder what the Sinking Parade is," said Uncle, as they took the other passage.

After a few steps they found themselves at the foot of an

immense escalator. It went up very slowly, and more and more people kept getting on to it.

At last they found themselves outside an enormous door of brown wood with the words 'Fish-Frying Academy' on it in brass letters.

Inside they had to pass through a turnstile where a little sharp-featured woman told them to turn out their pockets.

"We've had some bad thefts of fish lately," she said, "so we look as you go in and we look as you go out."

Uncle was a bit uncomfortable about the cat, for Goodman has an idea that it's all right to steal postage stamps and fish. He never takes anything else, but it seems impossible to cure him of these two faults.

However, there was no time to worry about this now, for a menacing roar came from the people behind who were having to wait while the One-Armed Badger's huge bale of goods was being examined.

"Seems to me this place is more bother than it's worth," said Uncle.

At last they reached the first department of the Fish-Frying Academy. A lot of boys were sitting at desks earnestly reading books and repeating sentences.

The teacher, a lean, anxious-looking man called Will Shudder, greeted Uncle.

"They're not allowed to touch a fish till they've been two years in this department," he said, "but now and then they get through in a year and a half. Here's one of our scholars who is getting moved up in seventeen months. Come here, Figby."

A pale boy, wearing an eyeshade and two pairs of spectacles, came up.

"Now Figby has got a good hold of the *theory* of fish frying.

He can repeat by memory nine hundred and eighty-one ways of cooking hake. Would you like to hear him?"

"No, thank you," said Uncle hastily, and they passed on.

Just as they were moving, Uncle heard a woman say:

"Look, there's Edgar in the crab-and-whelk class! Doesn't he look nice?"

She pointed to a small obstinate-looking boy who was busy writing in an exercise book.

"How's he getting on?" she asked the teacher.

"Well, ma'am," replied Will Shudder, "I'm sorry to say he's not doing too well. He actually brought a real crab to the class the other day, and offered to prepare it for the table. He said it only wanted turning out of its shell. Of course, we couldn't allow that, and now he's engaged in writing out a thousand times: 'Crab cooking is difficult, and takes months of careful study before one can even begin to understand it.' "

Just as he said this, the small boy took the exercise book and threw it on the floor.

"This fish-frying stunt is *soft*!!" he cried.

The teacher held up his hand in horror.

"Oh, I'm afraid that means expulsion!" he said. "You'd better come over to Professor Gandleweaver. He *may* give you another chance, but I'm very doubtful!"

"Oh Edgar!" wailed his mother. "After all the trouble we took to get you into the Academy!"

But Uncle stepped in.

"I think, madam," he said, "that I can give your son a part-time job in my kitchen, say for two hours a day."

"Oh sir!" said the woman. "This *is* good of you. Come out of the class at once, Edgar."

She was all smiles because it's a grand thing to work for Uncle.

They went on to a huge hall. In the middle of it, before a range, stood Professor Gandleweaver. He was a short stout man with shifty eyes, and he did not look very learned. Yet he must have been, for he had all sorts of diplomas pinned up on the wall behind the range.

In front of him, on a small table, was a single hake.

"Now, good friends," he exclaimed, in a pompous voice, "you're going to have a treat. I'm glad to see a bigger crowd than ever today, including the celebrated owner of the castle. I hope you didn't mind having your pockets turned out at the gate, but the fact is we've had some pretty bad cases of fish-stealing lately. A haddock vanished a few days ago, and yesterday a couple of herrings, though dead, managed to swim off!"

This was a joke, and was greeted with roars of laughter.

"But," continued Gandleweaver, "it's no laughing matter. Fish is dear. The expense of carrying on the Academy is heavy, and the cost of frying is always rising. However, you have come to see a bit of first-class frying, and I promise you you shall not be disappointed!"

He was just flourishing his pan before greasing it, when the cat Goodman darted upon the hake, and dashed out of the room with it.

Gandleweaver turned to Uncle with a furious look.

"You are a scoundrel, sir," he said. "You brought your cat here purposely to steal fish!"

Uncle waved his trunk in silence.

"I regret this incident, as much as anyone here," he said. "The cat who accompanied me has the unfortunate impression that fish and postage stamps are common property—"

There was a howl of rage from the crowd. They clearly didn't believe him. But Uncle waved for silence once again and continued:

"However, in order that you may suffer no loss, I will send you—" He shouted the next words:

"10 stone best hake,
7 stone plaice,
100 first-grade crabs
and 20 cod-fish.

"I think, after this," added Uncle, mildly but impressively, "that everyone will be satisfied."

Gandleweaver came forward all smiles, but Uncle turned haughtily away.

"I may say," he said, in tones of ice, "I shall take my own measures with my cat, but I am not altogether satisfied with conditions here!"

The crowd began to hiss, and, as Uncle didn't want a row, he decided to withdraw and take action later.

The moment he and his party got out of the crowd, they were

forgotten. The Professor had started frying a conger eel in an enormous pan, and this is one of his star turns; and nobody thinks about anything else when he does it.

Goodman was waiting outside the door of the Academy. As soon as he saw Uncle, he brought the hake and laid it at his feet in spite of screams of rage from the woman at the entrance.

"Be silent, madam," said Uncle. "I must remind you that this is my castle."

"Excuse my taking this fish, sir," said Goodman, "but that old Gandleweaver is a liar. Did you notice the pan of stale batter he was using? And his pockets were bulging with money. I never like a chap whose eyes are like a rat's. Now I've had a lot to do with rats—"

"Shut up," said Uncle. "You let me down by your conduct, and I've half a mind to punish you severely."

"Oh, you wouldn't do that, sir. I thought I was doing you a good turn, getting you out early. You'd never have stuck his lecture on frying. Why, it takes him half an hour to get the fat hot, and he talks and laughs the whole time. You'd never have the patience, sir!"

Uncle knew this was true, so he said no more. They took the hake back for supper, but it tasted horrible, so they gave it to Alonzo S. Whitebeard, who doesn't mind how things *taste* so long as they are free.

SEVEN

In the Library

THE next day Uncle decided to go with the Old Monkey to have a cup of coffee at Gasparado's Restaurant.

Gasparado's is situated in the market-place of Badgertown. It's rather a doubtful restaurant. Uncle doesn't know that customers are sometimes hit on the head, robbed and left to cool off in the little Italian garden at the side of the shop. He goes there occasionally simply because the top window overlooks the market-square, and is so well hidden that he can't be seen. That's an attraction to Uncle.

He ordered a bucket of special coffee with a cup for the Old Monkey. Gasparado brought it himself, and greeted them with an oily smile. "It's very good of you, sir, to patronize our quiet little house," he said.

Uncle only grunted. He doesn't like Gasparado much. Gasparado went away, and Uncle, after drinking his coffee, picked up

58

a paper called the *Badfort News*. He does not take this paper regularly, but when he comes across a copy in a café he eagerly reads it. This was what met his eyes:

ANOTHER OUTRAGE

We are horrified to find that the Tyrant of Homeward has added yet another to his long list of crimes. He went yesterday to the excellent Fish-Frying Academy of Professor Gandleweaver, and there carried out a contemptible theft. He took with him a degraded cat that he had specially trained to steal fish. This feline burglar seized a valuable hake from the Professor's table.

Uncle looked up from the paper with a frowning face that disturbed the Old Monkey. Just then they heard shouting and laughter in the square, and, throwing down his paper in disgust, Uncle looked out of the window. The Old Monkey ran to stand beside him.

What they saw surprised them.

There in the square were Beaver Hateman, Nailrod Hateman, and Sigismund Hateman. Beaver Hateman was playing a guitar, and Sigismund and Nailrod were singing a duet. They had a great portrait of Uncle on a board, with the newspaper cutting pinned on to it, and above it in red letters were the words:

THE WORLD'S TRICKIEST FISH-SNEAK

Crowds of people surrounded the singers. Flabskin and Jelly-tussle and many others of the gang were there to lead the responses. They called their song 'Question and Answer' and this is how it went:

Nailrod and Sigismund sang the first line, and the rest of the gang replied, while Beaver strummed his guitar and old Nailrod kept time on a drum.

> "Would you like to know just how to steal a fish?"
> "Yes, sir! Yes, sir! That is my wish."
>
> "Would you like to hear the trickiest way?"
> "Yes, sir! Yes, sir! Tell me today!"
>
> "How would it be to get a trained cat?"
> "Go on, sir! Go on, sir! There's something in that!"

They sang these verses and several more to a rather lilting tune, and then Beaver Hateman went round with a collecting box. People were laughing at his song, and humming it, and he seemed to be collecting a fair amount of money.

Uncle ground his teeth.

"If only I had a stone club!" he said.

Gasparado had been listening behind the door. Now he came in with a treacherous smile, and said:

"I have a ver goot stone club hanging up in de hall. It is curio that my broder brought me from Borneo. I hire him to you for thirty shillin'. It is dear because of de sentimental value!"

Uncle was desperate for vengeance, so he paid the thirty shillings and crept softly down the stairs.

All would have gone well, if that little wretch Hitmouse hadn't been on the look-out.

The moment Uncle and the Old Monkey emerged he shouted:

"Look out, here comes old Snorty!"

Before Uncle could swing his club the singers had vanished down a narrow entry, while Hitmouse dived down a drain.

Uncle looked round, and then tossed the club back into the restaurant with a haughty gesture.

"Pah!" he said to the Old Monkey. "Let's get away. The atmosphere is absolutely polluted."

They went back to Homeward, and there in the hall was the teacher from the Fish-Frying Academy, Will Shudder.

"I came to tell you, sir, that I've lost my job. The Academy has been closed down. All the boys rebelled after your last visit. They all want to work for you and think the fish-frying business is a wash-out."

Uncle rubbed his hands. All his annoyance was forgotten. He had been uneasy in his mind about the boys undergoing Professor Gandleweaver's fish-frying course.

"Well," he said, "I am glad to hear it. I may be able to find posts for some of the boys, and the younger ones can go to Dr Lyre's school. At any rate, they will be better there than at Gandleweaver's!" He paused, and then added: "I suppose Gandleweaver is still keeping up his fish-frying displays?"

"Oh, yes, he'll keep them up so long as he can get mugs to come and watch him. Between you and me, sir, he *can't fry*! He almost always burns the fish, and he uses abominably stale batter!"

"I can believe it," said Uncle. "Well, I think I can find you some useful work. How would you like to be a librarian? I've got a big library that wants classifying. A penny a week, free rooms and board!"

Shudder's weary eyes gleamed. He had long hoped for such a post.

"Oh, sir," he said, "what a wonderful chance! I promise I shall be systematic and work hard."

"The post's yours then," said Uncle, "and we might as well go and have a look at the library!"

They went there at once. The library is a most interesting place. It's quite near the dining-room, but hardly anyone goes there except Goodman the cat. Uncle himself used to be a great reader but since taking his degree he has read very little. However, he still orders books, and for some years these have piled up in the library. He orders at least a thousand books every year, and there is a vast pile there waiting to be put on shelves.

The building consists of a stupendous hall which goes all round the bases of four big square towers that are set about a lake. It's really four rooms in one, and the rooms are so big that if you want to go from one of them to the one opposite it's easier to row across than to walk round. A good boat has been provided for this. Although this lake comes right up to just below the windows, the hall is perfectly dry. It has books going up so high that you can't possibly see where the top rows are, but luckily there's a patent step-ladder with a chair at the back. Simply press a button and the chair soars right up to the ceiling, so that you can easily reach the topmost books.

The library walls are of a brown colour with rich red silk curtains. It looks very grand, but at the time when they saw it it was rather blocked up with great cases of books.

In it there are nine immense gas fires in fireplaces shaped like dragons. You light the gas, and the dragons become red-hot. It looks fine on a winter evening. It's evident that the place is honeycombed with secret passages, for there are all sorts of peculiar knobs and handles in places where there are no books.

In the middle of each of the four parts of the room is an ink fountain. A jet of ink shoots into the air from a black bowl, and falls softly back. It's a handy place for filling fountain pens and ink-pots. Also on a counter near the door there's a very convenient little stationery machine. This is shaped like a bear. Hit him in the right eye, and he shoots out a postcard from his mouth. Hit him in the left, and he shoots out a sheet of paper and an envelope. Hit him on the nose, and he shoots out a small flat box with ten sheets of paper and ten envelopes. And the funny thing is he never seems to run short.

Will Shudder had one look at the place and then began to cry.

"What's up?" said Uncle.

"Excuse me, sir," said Shudder, pulling himself together, "but I feel a bit upset with pleasure. I shall be perfectly happy here. I shan't need any wages—just a little of the plainest food, and I'll sleep among the books!"

"No you won't," said Uncle. "The Old Monkey will find you a room, and you shall have the wages I promised you, and eat at our table!"

"Oh, thank you, sir," said Will Shudder. "At that wretched academy I got no wages at all, and I had to live on stale fish and batter, and it was so frightfully dull!"

"Why did you stay then?"

"Gandleweaver promised me a partnership."

"It's high time you got out of all that. But, Shudder, there's one thing you might do for me here. I'm expecting a big attack from Badfort any day now. Just keep an eye open for anything unusual!"

They all went to have lunch after this. Shudder sat next to the cat. He tried to stroke him, but the cat is a very outspoken creature, and told him not to.

"Paws off!" he said. "You and I are going to be pals all right, but I can't bear being stroked. It makes me feel silly. I don't mind having my tail pulled. In fact, I rather like it. If you get hold of my tail and pull me along a smooth board, it's a real treat. Still, you and I will get on all right because we both like books. When

I was working for the wizard it got very tiring watching a rat-hole for hours, so I used to have a book by me and read by the side of the hole. It didn't prevent me catching 'em. Not a bit. I've even stunned 'em with a book before today!"

Soon after this Shudder and the cat went into the library for the afternoon. Shudder lit up the stoves and the place looked fine. He saw at once that it would take years to get the books thoroughly straight.

The cat took down a very interesting book and there was no sound except the faint turning of leaves, occasional slight mews, and the scratching of Shudder's pen.

There was a quiet almost sleepy atmosphere, but Goodman was wide awake. When an enormous rat peeped round the corner and began to nibble at the cover of a big book bound in leather, he got the surprise of his life. Goodman made one bound and was on him like a streak of lightning. He only just escaped and was ill for a long time afterwards.

EIGHT

They Call at Cadcoon's Store

T HERE was a little shop at the top of a hill near Uncle's that was called Cadcoon's Store, and Uncle had often thought of going there. The difficulty was to get away. There was so much to do at Homeward, and Uncle was practically sure that the Badfort crowd were about. Shudder told him that he was certain that he had heard someone swimming in the lake last thing at night when he went to shut up the library.

The cat Goodman had also found an empty Black Tom bottle on one of the sills.

All this made Uncle somewhat reluctant to leave his house, but one morning he received a letter.

It was from Cadcoon:

Honoured Sir,

I have long wished you to visit my store and sample my goods, but I know that your time is much taken up. However, I have received a threatening letter from Beaver Hateman, in which he says that he is coming today to obtain provisions from me free of cost.

As he will be safely away from your district, I suggest that you pay me a visit with some of your friends. I should like you to see me deal with that bandit.

Yours respectfully,

JOSEPH CADCOON

P.S. Try our Jumping Bean Rusks. Something new as a breakfast food.

"Good," said Uncle to the Old Monkey. "The way seems clear. I will take you and Gubbins. That will be enough, I think."

"What about me?" said the cat Goodman, who had been listening very eagerly.

"I think we had better leave you at home, my young friend, you might be stealing fish again!"

"Let him come, sir," said the Old Monkey. "He worked very hard yesterday with letters and parcels, and I haven't seen a single rat since he came."

In the end Uncle allowed him to go on condition that he behaved gravely and decently. They also took the One-Armed Badger. This time he was only allowed to carry empty cases and boxes, so that he could fill them at the store.

Cadcoon's Store was situated at the top of an extremely steep hill. It was really a wonder he got any customers, because it was very difficult indeed to climb up to the store. People often slipped in the winter and rolled down from the top to the bottom. Still he had a fair number of customers. His stuff was not very cheap, but it always had a peculiar rich flavour that made you want to taste it again.

They found it very hard work to get up the hill, but at last they reached the top, and paused for a moment to get their breath. Just ahead of them, on a sort of platform, stood Cadcoon's Store. It didn't look like a shop, but more like a house. It was very neat and had pretty curtains at the windows. These were made of panther-skin, and Cadcoon was very proud of them. From these bow windows you could look right on to the porch.

"If he's expecting Beaver Hateman I hope he's rubbed those windows with Babble-Trout Oil," said Uncle. "They just ask to be broken, sticking out like that."

"What's Babble-Trout Oil?" asked Goodman.

"Any glass rubbed with it is unbreakable," said Uncle. "Useful stuff."

"I'm sure Mr Cadcoon will have a good supply," said the Old
Monkey, "to protect his curtains."

The funny thing was that though Cadcoon's Store was noted
for good provisions the only food they could see as they stood in
the porch was one loaf of white bread on a shelf behind the front
door. Cadcoon soon came to the door. He was a neat, gentlemanly
man, and he welcomed them in and took them upstairs, where
there was a large room covering the whole top of the house and
with views to every side.

"I've been thinking out a nice meal for you," he said. "What
do you say to bread and butter?"

"Thank you," said Uncle, though he thought it sounded a little
on the plain side for visitors. He changed his mind though, when
he tasted it. This was real Cadcoon bread and butter. You took a
bite. It tasted like bread and butter, and yet there was something
special about it. You took another bite and your pleasure increased. The cat Goodman was provided with a large brown pan
of milk; it looked ordinary enough, but he drank it with the
liveliest satisfaction, purring loudly, and every now and then
shouting: "Splendid!"

While they were enjoying the unexpected flavour of these delicacies, Cadcoon said:

"I expect Beaver Hateman any time now, and I'm going to deal with him. I know, sir, that you are the best subduer of this bandit, but I would like you to have a little rest today. Settle down and enjoy yourselves. Here's another plate of bread and butter. I will be downstairs washing the works of my clock with very thin gruel while I'm waiting. The thing goes slow, and I have the idea that thin gruel squirted into the works may do some good."

He went downstairs, and for a few minutes all was quiet.

Then in the distance they heard heavy snorting.

Someone was coming up the slope.

They all moved to the windows, and very soon a hot red face appeared over the edge of the platform.

Beaver Hateman had come by himself for once. As you know, he usually brings many supporters. He soon reached the front door and banged the knocker down so hard that it seemed as if the wood must split.

Then he gave a mighty shout:

"Bring out food, the best you've got, and hurry up!"

Cadcoon pulled aside the panther-skin curtains and put his head out of a little side window.

"Where's your money?" he asked sharply.

"Money? Me? Don't be a fool!" Beaver Hateman leapt forward and seized hold of Cadcoon's nose.

"Now, you rascal," he yelled, "bring out those provisions or I'll twist your nose off!"

Cadcoon could hardly speak, but he managed to mutter in a stifled voice: "Release me a little, I can't speak!"

Hateman loosened his grip, and told him to say what he had to say quickly.

"I'll come to the door and hand you out a loaf of my special bread, Mr Hateman," said Cadcoon humbly.

Hateman was reluctant to let him go, but did so at last.

"I want more than a loaf," he said, "a lot more, and hurry up, you slimy viper!"

Uncle, the Old Monkey and Goodman saw Hateman bang his fists on the bow windows, but the glass was too well rubbed with Babble-Trout Oil to break.

Then they all hurried out on to the landing so that they could look down into the hall and see what happened when Hateman and Cadcoon met at the front door.

The first thing they saw was Cadcoon reaching for the large white loaf that stood on the shelf by the door.

With a lightning movement Cadcoon opened the door and flung the loaf at Beaver Hateman. It hit him with great force on the head and sent him spinning along the platform. As they watched he disappeared over the edge, and they could hear him bellowing and roaring as he rolled down the slope.

"Oh, sir," gasped the Old Monkey, "that's no ordinary loaf!"

He was right. As they found out later the loaf was made of wood skilfully painted to look like a crusty loaf.

Goodman was down the stairs and outside in a flash. He came scampering back from the edge of the platform to report.

"Beaver Hateman's picked himself up. He was rubbing his head and saying horrible things. Shouting them too. I've never heard such things. Do you know what he said about—?"

"That's enough, Goodman," said Uncle. "I don't want to hear his vile remarks! I only hope he has learned a lesson."

Then Uncle turned to Cadcoon.

"I am much impressed by your quiet efficiency," he said, "and now let us have a look at your store."

Cadcoon led the way. He keeps his food in iron safes to protect it from flies and bandits.

Uncle bought a lot of things including a number of boxes of Jumping Bean Rusks. The One-Armed Badger was soon so laden that Uncle did not think it safe for him to carry the provisions down the slope, so Cadcoon lowered them to him by ropes. They saw no further signs of Beaver Hateman and it was not long before they were home.

Late that evening Cadcoon sent them a little poem describing the day's adventures. It was beautifully written on violet parchment in yellowish ink, and was very long—at least twenty verses.

The Old Monkey began to read it aloud to the others.

"I was washing in gruel the works of my clock
    For the thing was inclined to go slow,
    When I heard at the door a thunderous knock
    And a voice bellowed loud: 'Bring out dough!'

"I went to my little side window and pulled
    My panther-skin curtains aside.
    A thumb and four fingers closed tight on my nose.
    'Bring me money—or grub,' the voice cried.

" 'Bring me sausage and cakes,' repeated that voice,
    'Bring me buns, or your nose I shall nip—' "

At this point Uncle began to snore. He does not like poetry, and he had had a very heavy day.

NINE

Cadcoon's Sale

IN THE early hours of next morning Uncle was awakened from a refreshing sleep by the Old Monkey.

"There's a big blaze, sir! I'm afraid that Cadcoon's Store is on fire."

Uncle bundled himself into a dressing-gown and looked out of the window. On the top of Cadcoon's hill there was a blaze that looked like an erupting volcano.

"That must be Cadcoon's Store," said Uncle. "It's doomed, that is quite clear. There is hardly any water on that hill."

As they watched, the flames grew higher and higher till they lit the whole countryside. Then there was a tremendous outburst of flames and sparks, and gradually the fire began to die down.

"Oh, sir, what can we do?" asked the Old Monkey, anxiously.

"We'll go and see if there is anything to be done for Cadcoon himself," said Uncle, "but the store has gone, I'm afraid."

While they were dressing, Cadcoon crept over the drawbridge. His neat suit was blackened, and his face woebegone and grimy.

"Oh, sir," he cried, as soon as he saw Uncle, "this is a sad night's work! Everything's gone up in flames. My panther-skin curtains gone! Not a rag left!"

It was too much for the little man, and he laid his head on the table and sobbed.

Uncle, however, was able to cheer him.

"We've got some panther-skin curtains in our furniture department and you can have them," he said.

Cadcoon was overjoyed. "Oh, sir, this is too good of you. Are you sure you can spare them?"

"Panther-skin curtains are rare," said Uncle, "but I can fix you up all right."

Thus encouraged, Cadcoon took an early breakfast, and Uncle gave him a glass of Sharpener Cordial. Then he began to look better.

"Somebody set it on fire," he said, "and I know who that somebody was. It was Beaver Hateman. But the difficulty is to prove it."

The cat Goodman, who had been rubbing himself against Cadcoon's legs and trying to comfort him, said quickly:

"It was Beaver Hateman, right enough. There's an old rat that brings his friends in from the country, and I thought I'd trace him home last night. D'you know where he lives? I will say he's got a first-class hole up there on a sunny hillside with a good view—"

"Go on," said Uncle.

"This hole is not far from your shop, Mr Cadcoon. I didn't want to climb that hill twice in one day, but I had to trace that wily old rat and stop him bringing his relations down to Homeward. In front of me, in the dark, I could hear heavy breathing, and soon I caught up with Beaver Hateman riding the Wooden-Legged Donkey and carrying a tin of petrol!"

"Ah, a tin of petrol!" said Uncle. "Useful evidence, Goodman!"

"But it doesn't prove anything and my house has gone!"

sighed Cadcoon. "Still," he said, cheering up a little, "the safes are still there and some of the food in them may be eatable, in fact freshly roasted. I think I'll have a sale, and with the money I get, and my savings, I'll start building again. I've got the panther-skin curtains, anyway, thanks to you. That's a good start."

Then he became downcast again.

"But how can we let people know in time?" he wailed.

"Leave it to me," said Uncle.

He turned to the Old Monkey.

"Ring up for the traction engine," he told him.

"But, sir, it'll never get up Cadcoon's hill."

"We'll take it through Badgertown to the foot of the hill—and keep sounding the hooter; and I will tell the crowd through a megaphone where we are going. I object to advertising," he added, "but this is a good cause."

They set off almost at once. The sight of Cadcoon, grimy and singed, on the traction engine beside Uncle filled the badgers with sympathy, and soon they were flocking up the hill to the smouldering ruins.

When Cadcoon unlocked his safes he found, as he had thought, that some of his food was splendidly roasted. The butter, of course, had melted and run about, but Cadcoon scooped up several buckets of it. It would be splendid for cooking.

Just as the crowd was eagerly bidding for the goods, Uncle heard the Old Monkey gasp:

"For shame!"

Uncle looked round and saw Beaver Hateman, Flabskin, and old Nailrod Hateman stroll coolly up.

"You take my breath away!" said Uncle. "Setting Mr Cadcoon's shop on fire and then daring to come and bid at his sale!"

"Who says I set the place on fire?"

"My cat Goodman saw you going up the slope towards the shop with a can of petrol last night!"

"Your cat!" hissed Beaver Hateman. "A nice witness! He's a common thief, a contemptible fish-sneak! All you've got is one thief as a witness. But I can bring scores, hundreds, to say I was nowhere near Cadcoon's last night! Come on, Flabskin, where was I?"

Flabskin scratched his head in a horrible sort of way and said: "You were down at Oily Joe's clearing out the till!"

"That's no good," said Beaver Hateman. "Let's have another

witness. Here's my father, dear old Nailrod Senior. Now you can believe a father when he speaks about his son, can't you?"

"I can believe *some* fathers," said Uncle.

"Come on, Dad," said Beaver Hateman. "What was I doing last night?"

Old Nailroad thought for a while.

"My son Beaver spent the whole of last night reading a good book," he said at last. "He only left his chair once, to get a lemon biscuit from the sideboard."

"You're lying," said Uncle indignantly.

"I can bring lots of witnesses!" said Beaver Hateman.

"I don't want to hear them," said Uncle.

All the same he wished he had one more witness to confirm Goodman's story. Just then the Respectable Horses appeared. There are four of them, three sisters and a brother, and they are always neat and polite. Their black coats looked very shiny against the ash and muddle of the burnt-out store.

"Ha, ha," said Hateman, smiling falsely at them, "here are my friends, the Respectable Horses. They won't believe the lies you've been telling about me."

"I'm sorry to say, Mr Hateman," said Mayhave Crunch, the eldest of the horses, "that what we have to say may be displeasing to you, but we must tell the truth."

"Why?" asked Flabskin.

"Shut up!" said Beaver Hateman, hastily.

"Continue, Mr Crunch," said Uncle.

"Last evening we were taking a pan of warm boiled oats to an elderly mule who is ill with influenza. He lives just below here. We found him shivering violently and with very little hay to warm him. He said that just before we arrived Mr Hateman had ridden up to his stable door and demanded dry hay. In spite of our

friend's protests Mr Hateman piled the hay on the back of the
Wooden-Legged Donkey and led the way to the store *carrying a
can of petrol.*"

"There's gratitude for you!" said Beaver Hateman. "I've never
been against you horses, never hit you or thrown anything at
you, and this is your return. All right! I've done with mercy
after this. I'm going to fight with the gloves off!"

"Have you ever had them on?" asked Uncle.

"Yes, I have," said Hateman. "I've never done half the bad
things I wanted to, but I'm going to start, and quickly too!"

Before Uncle could guard himself the ruffian had picked up a
bucket of warm melted butter and thrown it in his face.

Unfortunately Cadcoon happened at this moment to be in his
largest safe getting out some goods for the sale. Like lightning
Beaver Hateman slammed the door, shutting Cadcoon in. As he
made a rush for the path he also pushed Goodman into a vat of
warm vinegar, tripped up Gubbins, and threw a jar of salad-
dressing over Mayhave Crunch.

Then he was off, leaving confusion behind him.

Uncle was shouting and spluttering. Gubbins was staggering
about, half stunned. Poor Goodman struggled out of the vinegar
vat, his fur clinging to him. But the worst off was Cadcoon, shut
in the safe. He was pounding on the door and shouting.

"Attend to Cadcoon first," said Uncle. "The smell of all those
roasted provisions must be stifling. Unless we release him he will
be suffocated. Goodman, go as fast as you can to Cowgill's works
for the oxy-acetylene blowpipe!"

"Yes, sir," said Goodman, smartly, and was off down the path.

"The way he runs!" said the Old Monkey admiringly. "His
fur will be dry before he gets there!"

Uncle, regardless of his own discomfort, went to the safe and

tried to encourage Cadcoon. It's very hard to speak to anyone in a safe, the door fits so closely.

"How are you, my friend?" roared Uncle.

"I can hardly breathe!" came the faint reply.

"We've sent for Cowgill!" Uncle told him. "Have courage and eat a little of the provisions to keep up your strength!"

But Cadcoon did not answer. They thought they heard a thump inside the safe as if somebody had fallen over; then there was silence.

"This is very worrying," said Uncle, and added to the Old Monkey: "Is Cowgill in sight yet?"

The Old Monkey went to look over the edge of the platform and reported that Cowgill and his men were on the steep hill path already.

"But they're having an awful struggle with the equipment, sir," he said.

"Go and help, then," said Uncle, "and take Gubbins."

As soon as the blowpipe was hoisted on to the platform they set to work and the lock was soon cut out and little Cadcoon, very white and in a dead faint, was lifted into the fresh air.

There was no water so they had to fan him with their hats.

Luckily Uncle found he had a box of Faintness Producer for Burglars in his pocket. He put two tablets in Cadcoon's mouth and the little man opened his eyes almost immediately.

"Where am I?" he asked.

"You're all right," said Uncle, "and in your own home. Your own ruin, I should say."

"How did I get locked in the safe?"

"Need I say?" said Uncle. "It was Beaver Hateman."

When Cadcoon heard this, in spite of his weakness, he seemed to expand to twice his size, his hair bristled, and he dashed to the ground two great jars of pickled cabbage that were standing by. This seemed to relieve his feelings for he grew calmer and turned to Uncle.

"Sir," he said, "I owe you an apology. Once, I must own, when you kicked that man up I thought, privately, that you were a little hard on him, but now I see my mistake. You were too lenient, far too merciful."

Words failed Cadcoon. In spite of the medicine he was still weak.

"He will pay for his atrocious action," said Uncle; "and now let us all sit down and revive ourselves with a meal. Cadcoon, lie on that rug and have a drink of Sharpener Cordial."

In spite of everything they had quite a jolly meal. The air on the top of Cadcoon's hill was fresh and gave them a good appetite, and the food Uncle had bought at the sale tasted really splendid.

Next day they went on with the sale and it was quite a success. Cadcoon got enough money to start rebuilding, and he went to stay with Uncle till he felt really better.

TEN

They Go to Lost Clinkers

WHEN Uncle came downstairs a day or so later he found Goodman reading the paper, and also eagerly eyeing a wasp that was flying round the big treacle tub that stands in the middle of the table.

As soon as Uncle appeared he took a flying leap and jumped on to his shoulders, purring loudly.

"Good sport at Badfort this morning, sir," he said. "The police are there!"

"Not before time," said Uncle.

"Beaver Hateman's been having meals on credit at a little restaurant run by a chap called Winkworth. When at last Winkworth asked for his money Beaver Hateman and Flabskin dashed out, so he sent the police from Badgertown to arrest them. And there they are, twenty of them, great big chaps they are—"

"Don't talk so fast," said Uncle. "Calm down a little."

"Well, there they are waiting for him to come out. That's all, sir."

"They'll wait a long time," said Uncle. "But I tell you what, we'll have a day off to go exploring. It's pretty evident Beaver Hateman won't leave Badfort for a while, so we'll just have a trip I've long wanted to make, to Lost Clinkers."

The Old Monkey clapped his paws. He loves going to new places.

Will Shudder was glad to go because he wasn't feeling very well. One of the stoves in the library had started leaking and a day in the country was just what he needed.

There are cheap trips to Lost Clinkers on the Badgertown Railway, so Uncle sent Goodman to get the tickets and to inquire the time of starting. The tickets were only a penny each and this included lunch on the train. Not much of one—only watercress, melons and a few biscuits—but the badgers love these things.

"The stationmaster has put on a special trip for you, sir," said Goodman when he came back. "Seven hundred badgers are going on the afternoon trip, and he thought you might like a quiet look round before they arrived."

"Very obliging of him," said Uncle. "I shall not forget his thoughtful kindness. We'll start at once."

They didn't have to go to the Badgertown Station, for the stationmaster had the train run right up into the siding outside Uncle's lard department. So they all climbed in and glided off. When the ticket collector came round Uncle gave him three pounds to pay for the special train and also a threepenny bit for himself.

The scenery was very pretty at first. There were lots of woods, with great purple flowers as big as shields, and some ponds full of yellow fishes, but the nearer they got to Lost Clinkers the uglier it became.

Lost Clinkers is really an old deserted gasworks; it's not much to look at but the air there is very good. There were great piles of cinders and rubble and everything was black with soot. At last the train began to run beneath blackened arches and between bluish pools that looked as though they contained chemicals, and finally drew up in the very yard of the gasworks.

"I'm specially glad to come today, sir," said Will Shudder to Uncle, "because I have a friend living at Lost Clinkers—a writing master called Benskin. He gets a free room in the gasworks, you see."

"Rather an awkward place to get pupils, isn't it?" said Uncle.

"Yes, he has to travel round to other places giving lessons."

At first when they got out of the train they couldn't see anybody, but soon they found the writing master frying some small fish over a cinder fire.

Shudder introduced him to Uncle.

"I'm very glad to meet you, sir," said Benskin. "I've been intending to come to Homeward just in case there was someone who would like to take lessons in fancy and copperplate writing."

"Come by all means," said Uncle. "I shan't require you myself. My signature is well known and I don't intend to alter it. Most of my business letters and accounts are done by the Old Monkey and this cat."

The writing master looked deeply interested.

"That's the first cat I've ever seen that can write," he said.

"Then there's Cloutman here, a fair writer, but he holds his pen like a pistol. Gubbins is very slow. They could both do with a polish up."

"Oh, I'll come, sir," said Benskin eagerly. "I have to seize every opportunity. I earn my living through my writing desk. That reminds me, Shudder wrote a little poem about my work. I liked it very much and had it hung up in my office. Just have a look in. I should like you to see my specimens of fancy writing too."

Uncle went with him to the Gasworks Office. Benskin had his

writing desk in the window, which was a large one. There were some splendid specimens of his work. He can draw swans, deer and geese without taking his pen from the paper. He writes the most beautiful copperplate, and can sign his name with a sort of ornamental flourish that takes half a sheet of paper, all curves and bows. Hanging on the wall in a neat frame was the poem to which he had referred.

It was called 'Prepositions'. He read it aloud slowly to Uncle with great emphasis and making many graceful movements as he did so.

PREPOSITIONS

"He earned his beef *through* his writing desk,
  And toiled in the twilight dank,
  With pen of gold and flourish bold,
  A scribe of the loftiest rank.

"He kept his beef *in* his writing desk,
  And fastened it with a lock—
  A solid hunk of the savoury junk,
  With suet firm as a rock.

"He took his beef *from* his writing desk
  And laid on the lid his prize,
  While a haggard man to his window ran
  And looked in with envious eyes.

"He carved his beef *by* his writing desk,
  On the oaken window board,
  And with glittering steel, and fork like an eel,
  He served forth his flavourous hoard.

"He ate his beef *on* his writing desk—"

"What do you mean— 'fork like an eel'?" interrupted Uncle.

"He whirls it round and then wriggles it in, like this," said Benskin, demonstrating with his pen, "but you must admit, sir, that it's a good poem. Lots of people don't know what a preposition is. So, when I give writing lessons, I often give this poem as a copy, and so I teach writing *and* grammar at the same time."

The cat Goodman had been eagerly listening to this, and all at once he burst out:

"Oh, I think that's splendid, Mr Benskin. I've often wanted to learn grammar. I can read all right, taught myself at the wizard's. He got lots of letters from people, and, having rather bad sight, he used to call me in. 'Now, Goodman,' he would say, 'look at that letter. Tell me what that word is. Write it out, you fool, if you can't read it! Make a copy of the words!' So I found myself writing out words which I didn't know. It was more like drawing than writing at first. Then I learned to read a few of them. At last I learned to read jolly well, and Blenkinsop often got me to read him spells from his wizard's book, but grammar I never learned. It must be splendid!"

"Not half so good as writing," said Benskin. "Here, just let me see you sign your name."

The cat took the pen and signed his name in bold but rather spluttering letters, CANUTE GOODMAN.

"So that's your name, CANUTE?" said Benskin curiously. "I must say you write extraordinarily well for a cat, but not like me."

He took a fresh sheet of paper and a gold pen, and first wrote 'Canute Goodman' in exquisite copperplate. Then he surrounded the whole name with graceful flourishes, birds, flowers and scrolls. The cat watched him with its eyes nearly bursting out of its head.

"Oh, I should love to do it like that!" he said.

"You can learn," said Benskin, "if you try!"

"Oh, I'll try. You'll find me at it all the time."

Uncle was getting tired of this conversation, and here he interrupted.

"I have no objection," he said, "to my cat having a *reasonable* amount of education, but I don't want it to become a craze. He has heavy and responsible duties day by day, and I say to you, Goodman, don't overdo things. Don't get mad about things. Steady must be your motto."

Goodman seemed a bit over-awed, but this didn't last long, for he caught sight of a rat running along a beam in the gasworks, and rushed after it so fast that they could just see a white streak in the air.

Uncle smiled. "And now," he said, "we are here not on business but on pleasure. I propose first of all that we have lunch in the retort house."

It was nice and cool in the retort house, and the One-Armed Badger soon had ready a splendid lunch, including more than twenty bottles of ginger ale and raspberryade. When they had drunk these, Uncle threw all the empty bottles at a great iron pillar in the corner. Then they turned on a few taps. It was very interesting. One of them sent out a great flood of greenish, evil-smelling liquid at such a rate that they began to think they would be washed out of the retort house. Then it stopped, and from the tap came a long groaning sound mixed with whistles, and a loud TAP, TAP, TAP.

"There's someone in that tank!" said Uncle. They went and examined it but could find nobody. It was very mysterious. Then, all at once, Uncle noticed that the cat Goodman, who had been absent during lunch, had now turned up, and his fur was streaked with the green stuff.

"You rascal!" shouted Uncle. "You've been rapping inside that tank and trying to fool us!"

The cat blushed.

"Sorry, sir. I came across that tank when I was chasing the rat, and all at once it began to empty. When the water had all gone I thought it would be a bit of fun to groan and whistle and rap inside a bit. I only did it for fun, sir."

"Look here, Goodman," said Uncle, sharply, "this habit of joking is growing upon you; what you did wasn't funny at all! I thought for the moment that some unfortunate person had been put in that tank by Beaver Hateman. This sort of thing has got to stop!"

"I won't do it again, sir!" said Goodman meekly.

"You'd better not, and for a punishment you can go without lunch."

The cat looked hungrily at the remains of the feast but said nothing. However, the Old Monkey secretly gave him a meat pie, and he was soon rushing round again as full of beans as ever.

Then they walked over some slag heaps to a big reservoir and had a good swim. It was very interesting swimming there because there are great big pipes and iron ladders in the reservoir, and a big iron thing in the middle like a buoy. They all climbed on this and then paddled it round the reservoir. After this they climbed to the top of a rusty iron tower by means of a spiral staircase, and had some singing in the open air. They sang several choruses, and then Uncle cleared his throat and said: "I've half a mind to give you a solo."

Everyone was deeply interested in this, for Uncle had never sung to them before.

"Please, sir, do sing!" begged the Old Monkey, his eyes shining. He loves singing, even by the Badfort crowd; and now, to hear his idol Uncle sing – this was rapture indeed.

"How I'd like to hear you!" said Goodman, running round in circles to show how pleased he was.

"I'm not much of a singer myself," said Cloutman in a heavy dogged voice, "but a bit of really good solo singing makes me feel fine."

"It would be a great pleasure to a humble acquaintance, sir, if you would favour us with a song," said the writing master in his polite refined voice.

In the end Uncle was persuaded.

"Don't expect anything very great," he said. "I'm badly out of practice, and shouting at Hateman hasn't done my voice any good. However, to please you, I'll try."

Uncle has a very small singing voice. Everybody was surprised. It sounded so strange coming from such a big creature, and he sings in rather a mincing way, very different from his usual thundering tones. They were all amazed.

This was the song:

> "Flowers in my garden grow
> Of which gardeners brag;
> But the sweetest flower I know
> Is a daisy on the slag.
>
> *"Honour to the daisies*
> *On the slag-heap high;*
> *Let us sing their praises*
> *Till they reach the sky!*
>
> "They say the loveliest flowers cling
> Beneath an Alpine crag;
> But the sweetest flower I sing
> Is the daisy on the slag.
>
> *"Honour to the daisies—"*

The Old Monkey broke down at this point and was led out weeping, but he soon came back so as not to miss anything.

To the great delight of the whole assembly Uncle was persuaded to sing the four verses through three times more.

"Well," said Cloutman when, finally, he stopped, "I call that singing!"

"Singing," said Gubbins. "Sigismund Hateman is nothing to it!"

"Allow me to say," said the writing master, "that I have heard the greatest artists, but, without any flattery, I should put your singing by the side of that of Signor Maletti of Trieste, and I think the Signor would have to say that he was defeated!"

Uncle was very pleased at these comments, and he promised them presents when they got back.

"But where's Will Shudder?" he asked.

Shudder had not been well enough to join in the swimming or to climb the tower, but he had been lying on the top of a big slag heap near by and drawing the keen air into his lungs.

"I'm here, sir," he called down, "and I heard your singing; it sounded so faint and ethereal and fairy-like. It was really beautiful!"

Uncle glowed with pleasure and promised to give Shudder a wireless set when they got back. This seemed to make Shudder feel much better, and he was also delighted to hear that Uncle had invited the writing master to stay at Homeward for a few days.

By this time it was getting near sunset.

They were looking out from the top of the rusty iron tower when they saw the seven hundred badgers arriving from the excursion train which, as it was such a long one, had had to stop a little way down the track.

They were striding out and singing their marching song:

"On we go, watching the setting sun;
Tomorrow we will do it, if today it can't be done!"

A big badger was marching in front giving them the first 'On we go' in a tremendous bass voice.

"The afternoon trip doesn't give them much time," said Uncle, "but I suppose they can manage a hasty look round the gasworks, and a quick dip in the tank before they roll up for the train."

When it was getting dark the seven hundred took some collecting from all the corners of the gasworks, but at last they were all found.

Also the cat Goodman had done something to make up for his tricks in the empty tank.

While running after the rat he had found ten sacks of dog biscuits in a boarded-up room behind a furnace. Uncle left a note to say he would pay the owner in full if he presented himself at Homeward, and he distributed the biscuits to the badgers on the return journey. They were immensely pleased, and the train resounded with song and merriment till they pulled up outside Homeward.

As he had promised, Uncle gave good presents to all the members of his party.

Will Shudder spent the rest of the evening trying out his new wireless set. The worst of it was that he could only get Badfort. There is a wretched little broadcasting station on the roof of Badfort which seldom works, but it was going that night and Shudder heard the following:

News Summary (Copyright).

Weather: Rotten.

Base accusations were levelled today against B. Hateman
Esq., B.A., and a strong party of police from Badgertown
have placed themselves outside the main entrance of his
residence at Badfort. This unprovoked and grossly unfair
action has made Mr Hateman seriously ill, and he is at
present confined to his bed.

Public indignation runs high.

Mr Hateman asks us to state that, as he has heard that many
sympathizers desire to send gifts, these should be sent

c/o J. Jellytussle Esq.,
The Bathing Lodge,
Nr Badfort.

Ham, vegetables, biscuits, Leper Jack of good quality will
be acceptable; in fact anything can be sent, but not to the
front door please, as the police are still there.

ELEVEN

They Set Out for the Dwarfs' Drinking Fountains

NEXT day all still seemed quiet. In the library Mr Benskin was executing designs with his golden pen, and Goodman and the One-Armed Badger were watching him. The One-Armed couldn't write at all, but he was a most painstaking creature and eager to learn.

"It's about time I went to see the drinking fountains," said Uncle, yawning. "I've heard they're not being kept in very good repair. An ungrateful lot, those dwarfs. Sometimes I wonder why I bother with them. As Badfort is more or less besieged by police I think this is a good day to go."

Uncle is very proud of the 144 drinking fountains he erected for the dwarfs in Lion Tower when he first became rich. They are mentioned on page 11,564 of Dr Lyre's *History of Lion Tower*, only three pages from the end, and you will remember that there is a large painting of Uncle opening them in his hall at Homeward.

"Please, sir, I don't want to miss my writing lesson," said Goodman anxiously. "I'm having one after the One-Armed."

"Very well, you can stay," said Uncle, but he was a bit surprised. The cat was certainly mad on writing at the moment.

"Can Mig come with us, sir?" asked the Old Monkey.

"Good idea," said Uncle. "He's been stuck in the kitchen a good deal lately. And Will Shudder had better come too. He still looks rather pale."

While they were getting ready Butterskin Mute arrived with a large pumpkin and a couple of splendid beetroot under his arm.

"What about you, Mute?" asked Uncle. "Would you like a look at the dwarfs' drinking fountains?"

"Oh yes, please, sir," said Mute, delighted. "Can I bring my rake?"

"By all means," said Uncle. "We might find it very useful. For instance, if the fountains are choked up, a rake would be the very thing for removing rubbish."

Mute was pleased, as he doesn't feel really at home without a rake.

Wizard Blenkinsop happened to call to see them that morning, and when he heard what expedition was planned he suggested he might do some magic and find them a shorter way.

"Splendid," said Uncle. "The drinking fountains are a long way off, through Lion Tower. That's why I haven't been able to keep a proper eye on them."

Blenkinsop got out his pocket spell-book and turned to section 218.

How To Find A Short Cut to Any Given Place by Magic.
Tie a bundle of red leaves with ginkle-string. Then mix with ashes from a fire lit by a lunatic's aunt.
Salve.
Add wire from a green-eyed child's fish-hook.
Limmer.
Wash residue in tears of a broken-hearted goat, then stir in a kangle-pot with scob liver.
Take residue and lay it on a flat warm pavement. It will lie in the form of a rough arrow and indicate route.

"That's all very well," said Uncle; "but these things will take a good deal of getting together. 'Ashes from a fire lit by a lunatic's aunt.' I don't know such a person."

"Excuse me, sir," said Goodman. "Mrs Smallweed might do. I was in her shop the other day buying linseed. It was on a top shelf behind some rat-traps. Well, we got it down, and—"

"Oh, buck up," said Uncle. "Is she a lunatic's aunt or not?"

"Well, she's got a nephew who comes to light her fire and I heard her say to him, 'You're nuts, Willie.' "

"I suppose that'll do," said Uncle. "Hurry up and get some."

"What about my writing lesson?" asked Goodman.

"Look," said Uncle, "you're here to help me first. Writing lessons come second. Get those ashes, and no rat-catching or foolery on the way."

Goodman streaked off to Mrs Smallweed's shop which is half-way between Homeward and Badfort.

"Now," said Uncle, "what else do we want?"

"We've got red leaves," said Blenkinsop; "there are some on that tree over there, but I haven't got a ginkle-string to tie them with."

"What is a ginkle-string?" asked Uncle testily.

"A ginkle-string is a long stretched-out piece of rag that's been used for cleaning pots and pans."

"Well, that one's easy. Bring one from the kitchen, Mig!"

The dwarf Mig was off like a shot.

"Now what's next on the list? — Wire from a green-eyed child's fish-hook? That'll take a bit of finding."

"No, it won't," replied Blenkinsop. "It's a wizard's standard ingredient, and I always carry at least one with me."

He opened his pocket book, and took out a short piece of wire. "There you are," he said.

Uncle was now becoming interested. He had never done wizard work before, and it's very fascinating when you get into it.

"*Salve!* What's that?"

"Oh, that's a professional term," said Blenkinsop. "It means tie together loosely, roll in warm butter, and shake."

By this time Goodman had arrived back with the ashes, so

they were able to *salve*, and then, with the addition of the wire from the green-eyed child's fish-hook, to *limmer*.

Limmering takes a bit of doing.

You take all the things for the spell and put them in a cardboard tube. You then blow them out three times while stamping on the ground. It sounds simple, but it's got to be done at the exact moment. However, it was done at last, and the residue, a shabby-looking bundle, was ready to be washed in the tears of a broken-hearted goat.

The difficulty was to find such a creature. There were lots of goats around, but none of them looked broken-hearted. Even Nailrod Hateman's goat, which had good reason for misery, only looked fierce.

They were quite at a loss, till the cat Goodman, who knows everybody, said he knew of a little tender-hearted goat who grazed secretly on the lawn outside Homeward. He went out, gave her a small pinch and told her to blub, promising to reward her with a bundle of choice hay if she did so. She was soon blubbering away, though her tears were hardly enough to wet the residue thoroughly. However they dampened the bundle, and Blenkinsop thought that would do.

Then they needed a kangle-pot. Blenkinsop had two or three at home, but it was too far to go and fetch them.

"I came across a pot in the library the other day, sir," said Will Shudder. "*It* looks to me remarkably like a kangle-pot."

"Please fetch it, Shudder," said Uncle.

A kangle-pot is a small red pot with leather handles, and with curious figures engraved on it.

"Oh, that's a first-class kangle-pot," said Blenkinsop in a discontented voice when he saw it. He was rather jealous, for kangle-pots are extremely scarce, and yet absolutely necessary for wizard work, and this was a unique specimen.

The next stage of the spell was a hard one.

A scob is a savagely biting fish, eaten only by the Badfort crowd. To get scob's liver seemed very difficult.

"Won't the spell work without scob's liver?" asked Uncle.

Blenkinsop laughed bitterly.

"Really, sir, I'm surprised you should ask such a question. It shows how little you know about wizard work. We might manage at a pinch without ginkle-string or red leaves, but never, never, never without scob's liver."

"I think I can buy some," said Goodman. "I'm not certain, but I'm nearly sure."

"Here's sixpence," said Uncle, "and hurry."

Goodman ran so fast that you could hardly see him at all. He went once more to Mrs Smallweed's. She's a good friend of the cat and they often have a gossip together.

"I want a pound of best scob's liver," said Goodman, putting the sixpence on the counter.

Mrs Smallwood held up her hands in horror.

"Oh, Mr Goodman," she said, "you don't think I sell that, do you?"

"Yes, I do," said Goodman. "When I was here a few minutes ago I saw a parcel labelled 'Badfort' and smelling of fish. It was scob, now, wasn't it?"

"Well, of all the cheeky cats! You are a bold-faced thing!" said Mrs Smallweed. "All right, I admit it. I do sell scob occasionally, but you mustn't tell anybody where you got it. It wouldn't do my business any good. Promise now."

"All right, I promise," said Goodman, and he seized the parcel of scob and rushed back to Homeward.

"Where d'you get it?" asked Uncle, curiously.

"Sorry, sir, I can't tell you. I promised not to. Hope you don't mind. It's proper scob's liver. I know about fish, and it's got a sort of bitter taste—"

"Stop talking," said Uncle, "and hand it over."

They were all ready now for the spell, but it had taken such a long time that they decided to have lunch first.

After a substantial meal, during which the wizard kept boasting of his skill, they went back to where Cowgill had already warmed the pavement with his oxy-acetylene blowpipe.

Blenkinsop was in his element. He stirred in the liver and threw the 'residue' on to the warm flat pavement. It lay in the form of a rough arrow. Suddenly it moved, became longer, and pointed directly at a massive stone wall.

"That's the place," said the wizard.

They tried to move some of the stones. Then they hammered and pushed, and even thrust knives into the crevices, but all to no purpose.

At last Uncle, who had been growing impatient, ran at the wall and gave it a great kick.

TWELVE

They Reach the Fountains

Uncle's foot must have landed exactly on a secret spring for, all at once, with a rumbling sound, the wall slipped sideways on rollers, and before them stretched a short, well-lighted passage.

"There you are," said Blenkinsop. "I knew it would work!"

Uncle said nothing. He thought it had taken rather a long time to do the spell but he was pleased to have made the opening kick.

This really was a short way to the fountains, for when the party got to the end of the passage all they had to do was to lift a plain wooden handle. A door opened, and there, before them, were fourteen of the drinking fountains.

They were very fine. Made in marble, each one was carved with an elephant's head from the mouth of which water gushed. Uncle soon saw that some of the outlets must be choked up, for water was running over the marble rims of the basins. But that was not the worst thing. To his horror he saw that one of the marble mouths had been actually boarded up, and a shabby hut had been built in the dry reservoir beneath.

Over it was erected this sign:

YOUR SYD

Mends clocks, watches and windows, boils eggs and soup, does family washing ($\frac{1}{2}$d. per doz. pieces), knocks up workers at any given hour, frames pictures, wheels out invalids, trims hedges and hair, shaves beards.

YOUR SYD

Also sings at concerts, tans leather, teaches exhibition dancing, and washes dogs and cats.

YOUR SYD

Has the best house for dwarfs' boots. A special line
in dwarfs' baby shoes. Difficult to get at most stores,
but YOUR SYD has a large stock from Size 1 upwards.

P.S. Something New. High-heeled shoes for short
dwarfs. Add at least an inch to your height.
Why be downhearted?

"Oh, sir," said the Old Monkey, "fancy setting up shop right
in one of your fountains!"

Uncle motioned for silence and peeped into the hut. Inside was
a thin man doing some washing in a small zinc bath. The clothes
he was washing were so exceedingly small that they must have
been dwarfs' baby clothes.

"Hardly bigger than postage stamps, this lot!" he was sighing.
"I'm sick of this job!"

He looked up, saw Uncle looming outside the doorway, and
jumped violently.

"I am Uncle, the owner of this castle," said Uncle solemnly.
"I must ask you why you have the effrontery to set up a trading
store in the bowl of one of my fountains?"

"There wasn't anywhere else," said Syd, trembling. "I've got
to make a living somehow. I ... I ... didn't stop the fountain up,
sir. It was done before I got here!"

"A miscreant's work!" said Uncle. "However, I can see you
are an enterprising man, willing to do anything. Have you got a
telephone?"

Syd looked like crying, but he pointed, with a soapy hand, to a
kiosk over by the wall.

Uncle rang up Cowgill and told him to come at once with men
and materials.

"Come by the route through Lion Tower; don't try the wizard's short cut," said Uncle before he put down the receiver.

Then he went back to Syd and told him that he had sent for his engineer Cowgill, and that a good wooden hut would be put up for him near the fountains.

"In return for this," said Uncle, "I wish for some information about the drinking fountains. They are meant for the good of the dwarf community and I can see they are not being cared for, or even used. Why is this?"

"They run with poisoned vinegar, sir," said Syd.

"Poisoned vinegar!" trumpeted Uncle.

Everybody was shocked. Poisoned vinegar is used by the Badfort crowd to throw in people's faces and make their eyes smart. Although it doesn't actually poison people, one drop of it can make a whole tank of water bitter.

"The first taste is enough to stop you drinking any more," said Syd. "It's all right for washing, though."

"This must be looked into at once," said Uncle. "Whoever is doing this must be punished most severely. Let me see, the fountains are fed from a tank reservoir above. How can we get up there?"

"There's an iron ladder, but it's padlocked," said Syd, "to stop the dwarfs' children from getting up."

Uncle, fortunately, had brought the right bunch of keys and they were soon up on a marble platform above the fountains.

This platform had a battlemented parapet all round it, and in the middle a huge tank reservoir with channels running from it to each of the fountains.

"Look at those, sir!" said the Old Monkey, pointing to ten little kegs which lay inside the parapet, nine of them empty and thrown on their sides, the tenth full and standing upright.

On each keg was a label which read as follows:

SNIPEHAZER'S VINEGAR (concentrated)
This preparation is undoubtedly the best on the
market. It is made with scrupulous care in our
laboratory and is absolutely pure.
For making drinking water bitter bore a small
hole in keg and set on edge of reservoir.
Use only Snipehazer's Vinegar. The genuine
article is made solely by T. Snipehazer (Wizard).
Do not accept imitations.

"Have you seen anybody up here?" asked Uncle, controlling
his anger with difficulty.

"Only the man from the waterworks who comes every Thursday afternoon," said Syd. "He comes to check the washers. All
you can see from below is his bowler hat."

"I should like to point out, sir," said Will Shudder, "that this
is Thursday afternoon."

"Good, good," said Uncle ominously, "we will take a look at
this man from the waterworks."

"That's the way he comes," said Syd, "through that lift."

They had not long to wait before they heard the clanking of the
lift door and a short man in a thick overcoat and a bowler hat
came out. He was carrying a large gimlet. One look at the large
projecting ears was enough.

"Ha!" said Uncle to the Old Monkey. "It's Goatsby!"

"What a good thing we came, sir," whispered the Old Monkey.
"No wonder we haven't been hearing the fountains praised
lately!"

As soon as Goatsby saw Uncle and his friends he turned pale,

but he pocketed the gimlet hastily, and made a ghastly attempt at politeness:

"Oh, good afternoon, sir," he said. "What a surprise to see you here!"

"I may say the same about you. What are you doing here?" asked Uncle, gravely.

"I like it here," said Goatsby. "I come here for peace and quiet. I sit down by the side of this bubbling pool and think."

"The reservoir of a drinking fountain is not exactly a public lounge, is it?" asked Uncle.

"It makes me happy to be here," said Goatsby, with an utterly false laugh.

He was playing for time.

If it had been possible he would have dashed into the lift and vanished, but Uncle, Will Shudder, the Old Monkey, and Mute, his rake held menacingly high, barred the way and advanced towards him.

Goatsby dared not take his eyes off them, but at last, in spite of his thick overcoat, he turned to make a run for it. As he did so he stumbled over one of the empty kegs. The others lay beyond it.

He fell with arms outstretched across them, with such force that they ran forward like the wheels of a roller skate and tipped him head-first into the reservoir. He fell in with a mighty splash, sank and then came up spluttering.

"Let him flounder for a bit," said Uncle, "and then pull him to the side with your rake, Mute."

This was done, and the last they saw of Goatsby was a sodden figure with water dripping from his projecting ears crawling into the lift.

"That makes me feel better," said Uncle.

He gave instructions for the fountains to be properly cleaned, and for Syd to be moved into the new hut. This was to be rent free on condition that he sent Uncle an account of the state of the drinking fountains every month. This he promised to do, and Uncle went home in high spirits.

THIRTEEN

Skinner's Hotel

WHEN they got back from the drinking fountains Uncle made a new resolution. As he slowly drew up into his trunk a quart of hot coffee from the tub at his side, he said:

"I shall have to give more oversight to things, you know. The state of those drinking fountains was a disgrace, and look at this—"

He threw across the table a copy of the *Badfort News*.

"Oh dear," said the Old Monkey, "has that paper-boy made a mistake again bringing that awful paper here? I've told him again and again!"

"I will be forced to take some action about this vile rag before long," said Uncle. "That is quite clear."

The Old Monkey read:

Our readers will be saddened to hear of another outrage by the Dictator of Homeward.

One of our esteemed citizens, Mr Laurence Goatsby, having heard of the disgraceful state of certain drinking fountains in Homeward, recently made his way there carrying a small keg of disinfectant, with which he hoped to make the fountains usable again. When he arrived on his errand of mercy he found the Dictator waiting for him. The latter made some offensive remarks and Mr Goatsby quietly tried to leave.

He was at once surrounded by a menacing crowd, some of them bearing lethal weapons. In an effort to escape with his life Mr Goatsby unfortunately tripped and fell into the fountain reservoir, and has been suffering since from shock and a severe cold.

We call on all citizens to rise and resist to the death—Uncle, the fierce fat fool of Gangster Castle, Liar County, Robber Country, Taken-in-and-done-for-World.

"Oh sir, I'm ashamed to read it!" said the Old Monkey, almost in tears.

Uncle threw the newspaper into the fire with a contemptuous gesture.

As it was blazing up, the cat Goodman skidded into the room. He was in such a hurry that he dashed himself against Uncle's legs.

"Look where you're going!" said Uncle, still rather cross after reading the *Badfort News*.

"Sorry, sir," said Goodman, "but I was rather excited. What d'you think – a new hotel has just been opened, the Skinner's Arms!"

"Where?" asked Uncle.

"In Skinner's Lodge, that big old house between Badfort and Badgertown. You know all the doors and window frames have been torn off for firewood by the Badfort crowd."

"Yes, I do know. It was a good house, and lately it's been an eyesore," said Uncle. "To have it done up and made into a good hotel is a splendid move. Who's behind it?"

"A rich man called Battersby," said Goodman, who, as usual, knew everything. "Oh, sir, it's going to be wonderful! There's to be a palm court – and a silver ping-pong room and very cheap meals."

Uncle and the Old Monkey were deeply interested.

"I may as well go and stay there for a night or two," said Uncle, "to make sure it is being run on proper lines and is a benefit to the neighbourhood. I am determined to keep a general eye on things."

The Old Monkey was very pleased. A rest from housekeeping for a day or so would be a treat. He went off smiling to get lunch ready, but was soon back to say there was a visitor.

"He comes from the Skinner's Arms, sir," said the Old Monkey. "He's very polite, I must say."

"Show him in," said Uncle.

A shabby leopard came in, bowing rather humbly. Across his breast he wore a flashy blue-and-gold streamer which read: 'Skinner's Arms. Help yourself from the Silver Soup Stream. Runs night and day.'

"Ah, a soup stream," said Uncle, who loves a novelty of any kind. "This seems promising."

"Oh it is, sir," said the leopard, "and I'd be most grateful if you could see your way to make a firm booking. I get commission on each one, and to tell the truth I need every penny. I've got rather a big family, sir."

"You can book a couple of rooms for tonight," said Uncle, "for myself and the Old Monkey."

"What about Goodman, sir?" asked the Old Monkey. "He told us about the Skinner's Arms first, you know."

"Very well, he can come as long as he sleeps in your room," said Uncle.

So it was settled, and the leopard, departed looking much happier as Uncle had given him a keg of salt beef for his large family.

At six o'clock that evening Uncle mounted the traction engine. He left Cloutman and Gubbins in charge of Homeward, with Captain Walrus on call.

When they arrived at the Skinner's Arms they found hundreds of badgers, who had been attracted by the new spectacle, camped round the hotel. The old house had been much brightened up with new paint, and coloured lights, and flowers in tubs. The porter, a smart young bear, seized Uncle's luggage and led them into the lounge. This was rather fine. It was painted blue and decorated with gold circles.

"Where's the manager?" asked Uncle.

"There's Mr Battersby, sir," said the bear.

Mr Battersby came out of his office. He was a fairly tall man who wore dark glasses and what looked like a rather tight wig of red hair. Uncle felt he had seen him before somewhere, but where?

"Your appearance here, sir," said Battersby, making a sweeping gesture of welcome, "reminds me powerfully of an experience I had in a hotel in Tokyo. We were all in the lounge, bored and listless, when a whisper went round, 'Sir Thomas Tompkinson is here.' In a moment, all our dullness was gone, for Sir Thomas was noted as a good companion, a keen wit, a splendid sportsman, and, above all, for his utter absence of swank. One young man said to me, 'I could hardly bear to go on living, but now Tommy's back I'll try again!'"

This speech was listened to eagerly by a number of badgers who had managed to get into the lounge. Uncle couldn't help feeling rather gratified.

"Thanks, Mr Battersby," he said. "I'll try to live up to your description. May I see my rooms now?"

"This way, sir," said Battersby and called down the passage: "Moses, blow the trumpet of welcome!"

A lean fox began to blow into a small brass trumpet.

Mr Battersby clapped his hands and called:

"Agnes, unroll the Gold Carpet of Welcome!"

A small fat woman rapidly unrolled what looked like a yellow stair carpet, and Uncle tramped down it feeling a little embarrassed. Goodman scampered along behind, his white coat looking splendid against the yellow carpet.

Uncle's room was large and spacious, and on one wall was a huge enlargement of a photograph taken years before of the opening of the dwarfs' drinking fountains.

"Very well chosen," said Uncle.

Soon they heard a loud smashing noise.

"Mr Battersby smashes a large jug every evening to show dinner is ready," said Goodman. "Isn't it splendid?"

"Remember we are here on a visit of inspection, Goodman," said Uncle. "Your admiration should be moderate in tone."

All the same there was a lavishness in this act which appealed to Uncle, and he made up his mind to try one day soon having an even larger jug broken to announce dinner at Homeward.

They went down to the dining-room eager to see the much-advertised silver soup stream. There it was, a silver channel running round the table filled with hot soup, which was kept moving by a number of small electric paddles. Everybody took as much as he wanted by dipping a serving mug into the stream.

The help-yourself method also applied to the gigantic cooked fish which lay on a silver platter which stretched the full length of the table. You just reached forward and took what you wanted.

"This is splendid, sir," said the Old Monkey, dipping his mug into the soup stream for the third time. As for Goodman he was in raptures, having, for once, as much fish as he could eat.

Uncle's pleasure in these arrangements was rather spoiled by the sight of a mysterious person at the other end of the table. He had propelled himself to the table in a wheel-chair, and his head was swathed in bandages. But he seemed to have a good appetite. He drank mug after mug of soup with a gulping noise that was distinctly unpleasant.

"Who is that?" Uncle asked Battersby, who had come in to see if all was going well.

"That's Mr Bateman, our permanent guest," said Battersby. "He's an invalid, but very brave."

"He doesn't look much like an invalid to me," said Uncle, "and I don't like the way he keeps dipping that mug into the soup."

"It's running away from you, sir," said Battersby.

"Yes, I dare say," said Uncle, "but it comes round my way afterwards."

Because he found the manners of his fellow guest so unpleasant Uncle was glad when dinner was over.

Outside his door he found a group of musicians. One had a bassoon, one a flute, while a dwarfish creature, dressed in a kimono, was playing a zither. They all began to sing a song when Uncle appeared.

"We love to hear of Uncle's deeds,
    He makes us feel so glad;
    His bounty makes the poor man rich,
    And fills with joy the sad.

"How vast his stores of ham and lard,
    How huge his vats of oil ... "

It went on for about twenty verses, and still there seemed no prospect of it coming to an end.

"Thank you, friends," said Uncle, "for your singing. I'm going to bed now, but you can go on all night if you like."

He gave them some money and closed the door of his room.

"Now for bed," he said.

The Old Monkey was there to make everything comfortable, and he turned on the bedside lamp. The moment he did so it exploded with a loud report.

This made Uncle jump and he sat down rather hurriedly on the bed.

There was a cracking noise, and at once the bed legs began to go through the floor. The boards were flimsy and worm-eaten, and before Uncle could get up he had crashed, with the bed, through a jagged hole in the floor into the room below.

The bed took some of the force of the fall as its legs collapsed under it, but he fell with a nasty jar.

Sickening clouds of plaster and dust filled his nose and eyes.

Trumpeting loudly with rage, and half-blinded, he took some seconds to see that in falling he had bowled somebody over, and that a huge roll of bandage was looping and unrolling along the floor. It only needed one glance at the sack suit and huge feet to tell Uncle who the soup-drinking invalid had been.

"So it was you, Beaver Hateman!" shouted Uncle, hurling a bed-leg at him. "No wonder the food stuck in my throat!"

Hateman hopped on to the window-sill. "Thanks for falling on me, you fat old barrel of lard," he said. "You've given me a good idea which I shall use to bring about your downfall—and soon!"

Then he vanished, laughing hideously.

The Old Monkey and the cat Goodman were looking down anxiously through the hole in the ceiling.

"Oh, sir, are you hurt?" asked the Old Monkey, with tears in his eyes.

"Not severely," said Uncle, "but my suspicions about this place have now been fully confirmed. Go to the office, ring up for the traction engine and ask for my bill."

"I'll help you brush yourself clean, sir," said the cat Goodman, jumping through the hole on to the wreckage. "I'm good at that."

When Uncle and Goodman went into the lounge Battersby came out of his office to meet them.

"I'm very sorry to hear you have had a slight mishap, sir," he said. "Another room is, however, being prepared."

"I am not staying. Your floors are unsafe," said Uncle.

"Not for persons of ordinary weight, if you will excuse my saying so," said Battersby, smiling odiously.

"If you run a hotel a person of any weight must be safe on any floor," said Uncle. "My bill, please."

Battersby went into his office and brought out a long sheet of parchment, very neatly made out.

Uncle took it, frowning, and began to read; as his eye fell on one item after another he felt his temper mounting.

Dr to Skinner's Arms Hotel

	£	s.	d.
Gesture of welcome	1	0	0
Relating complimentary anecdote	3	10	0
Trumpet of welcome	5	0	0
Putting down gold carpet	10	0	0
Obtaining and hanging photograph of dwarfs' drinking fountains	15	0	0
Dinner (for three persons)		3	6
Serenade outside bedroom	100	0	0
Two rooms for night (1 single, 1 double)		2	6
Repairs to bedstead	105	0	0
„ „ bedroom lamp	10	0	0
„ „ „ floor	214	0	0
	463	16	0
Less discount for distinguished visitor			2
	£463	15	10

With a great effort Uncle kept control of himself. Then he tapped the parchment.

"Explain this monstrous bill!" he said, his trunk waving to and fro, in the way it did when he was really angry.

"It's quite moderate," said Battersby. "Dinner 3s. 6d., two rooms 2s. 6d. – for three people, mind."

"This bill," said Uncle, "is a ramp!"

"A ramp? What is a ramp?" asked Battersby.

"A ramp is an attempt to get money by false pretences," said Uncle. "I refuse to pay, of course."

"Indeed," said Battersby, with a rascally smile. "This will look well in the *Badfort News*."

Then Uncle noticed that the little creature in the kimono who had been playing the zither outside his room was sitting at a coffee-table writing on what looked suspiciously like a hating book.

"I see, you've got their reporter here!" said Uncle.

"Hitmouse!" hissed Goodman.

"I am not afraid of anything that may be said in that scurrilous rag," said Uncle. "And I will make sure a strong article warning people about this hotel goes into the *Homeward Gazette*."

"Oh nobody reads that boring old paper!" said Battersby.

"Meanwhile," said Uncle, "as I am unusually heavy I will send workmen to repair the bed and ceiling. For the rest I give you two pounds – and that's the lot."

Battersby now lost his temper completely.

"You'll go to prison for this!" he yelled.

At the sound of his rasping furious voice a terrible suspicion seized Uncle. Goodman must have felt the same, for he suddenly jumped on to Battersby's shoulder and pulled off the tight red wig. At once a pair of huge ears flopped out.

"Goatsby!" said Uncle, breathing hard. "So it was you, Goatsby, trying once more to defraud me!"

"You're defrauding me!" Goatsby was now nearly beside himself. "You'll get six months in prison for this! No, six years—*sixty!*"

"Perhaps you have forgotten," said Uncle in grave tones, "that I am the chief magistrate in this area. Can you see me sentencing myself?"

Seeing that he was likely to be involved in a vulgar struggle if he stayed longer Uncle made his way to the traction engine and they rode home.

FOURTEEN

On the Underground

IT WAS a dim winter afternoon, and Uncle was feeling slightly depressed. The morning had been quite prosperous. He had had some large cheques for maize, and had been asked by the King of the Badgers to open a sale of bananas and coconuts in aid of distressed badgers. He likes opening sales because it gives him a chance of wearing his best purple dressing-gown and elephant's gold-studded boots.

These were cheering things, but on the other hand the *Badfort News* had printed an utterly false description of his visit to the Skinner's Arms.

It had been headed: A MEAN MAGNATE.

And this is what it had said in smudgy black type:

The Dictator of Homeward Castle has a new line in crime. He stays at good hotels and refuses to pay his bills. A fine example to us all!

Yesterday he went to Mr Battersby's new establishment, the Skinner's Arms, and when presented with a modest bill refused to pay. In addition he conducted himself like a surly, ill-bred madman, breaking a lamp and bed and smashing through a floor.

When the long-suffering Mr Battersby told him that the only alternative to non-payment of bills was prison, he calmly remarked that he was the local magistrate and he wasn't going to sentence himself.

Now we know what injustice really means! Rise in thousands! Surround Uncle's mouldy castle and burn it to the ground!

It was irritating how many people had read this, while hardly anybody seemed to have seen Uncle's truthful account in the *Homeward Gazette*.

He was brooding on what steps he should next take against the Badfort crowd when the Old Monkey led in the little dwarf Rugbo who keeps a small grocery shop on the top of a high tower called Afghan Flats, near where Uncle's aunt, Miss Evelyn Maidy, lives with her companion, Miss Wace.

This dwarf was gulping with rage so that he could hardly speak. At last he said:

"Sir, you must come and help us. We are being robbed, *robbed*, ROBBED!"

"Wait a bit," said Uncle severely. "If I remember rightly you put a frog in my aunt's milk jug when I was visiting her some time ago."

"I'm sorry about that," said Rugbo, "but Miss Maidy got her own back—and more, sir. I can feel her umbrella still."

"My aunt," said Uncle, with a steady look at the little man, "took strong and effective measures to deal with an abominable action. Still, I am always ready to help sufferers from injustice. You may state the nature of the outrage."

"Outrage is a good word. That's just what it is, sir. They've put up the fares on the Underground!"

"What Underground? I know of no underground railway in this castle."

"You don't know the Dwarfy-Dwarftown Line from Number 1 Tower to Number 10 Tower?" Rugbo was plainly astonished.

"I don't know every corner of this castle of mine," said Uncle, "but wherever there is wrong-doing I make it my business to be there. I will examine the rise in fares and see if I consider it just."

"Oh, sir," said Rugbo, calming down a little, "thank you. I know you'll take my side."

"We shall see," said Uncle, and turned to the Old Monkey.

"Tell the One-Armed Badger to get ready," he said.

"Here he is, sir," said the Old Monkey, eagerly.

There seemed to be a sort of bale in the doorway. It was the One-Armed bowed to the ground with necessities for an expedition.

"Tell Cloutman and Gubbins to come. That'll be enough, I think."

Just then the cat Goodman appeared wheeling a small trolley filled with stone clubs.

"Oh, sir, look," said the Old Monkey. "Goodman will have to come."

So Uncle let him come.

"A stone club might be very useful," he said. "At any rate let us go and see this railway. But, mind you," he added looking at Rugbo sternly, "you will suffer if I find you have led me on a false trail."

"What you see, sir," said Rugbo, earnestly, "will make your hair stand on end."

"Lead the way," said Uncle.

Rugbo led them along a stone passage they had never used before. This led to a steel gallery, and at the end of this was a lift which seemed to go down, down, down a long way into the ground.

When the lift stopped and the door slid open they found themselves in the booking hall of the dwarfs' Underground Railway.

What a booking hall! The members of Uncle's party were amazed, for the place was as large as a football ground and the walls went up so high they were lost in a blue mist. And it was packed with indignant dwarfs.

In front of the booking office, where the crowd was thickest, there appeared to be a single mass of flattened dwarfs. And the

yell of rage that was going up from them was so loud that ordinary speech was impossible.

"You see what I mean, sir!" screamed Rugbo.

Uncle nodded gravely, and motioned to the Old Monkey to go and read the notice which was just being put up. There is nothing the Old Monkey enjoys more than running to and fro over the heads of a tightly packed crowd. He ran to the notice-board so quickly that he hardly seemed to touch their heads. He paused, read the notice, and was soon back to report.

"It says that the fare between each station has been increased from one to one and a half bananas, sir!" he shouted into Uncle's ear.

"Get some bananas out of the pack," Uncle told the One-Armed. "We will take a ride on this railway and see what it is really like."

A rather greasy old wolf was acting as banana collector and porter.

"Why has the fare been increased?" Uncle asked him.

"Wages has riz," he said, "or supposed to. Mine's the same *and* too small."

Rugbo had left them in the booking hall, for he had to get back to his shop which he had left in charge of a young errand boy who was very apt to help himself to biscuits and raspberryade, but the rest of them got into a first-class compartment. Almost at once the train started and ran through a tunnel to Number 2 Station. Here the platform was so packed with travellers it was a wonder they weren't pushed on to the line. As it was the train seemed to pass within an inch or so of their stomachs.

Seeing Uncle, the dwarfs avoided his compartment, but the overcrowding in the rest of the train was terrible.

"There are twenty under each seat, and at least fifteen in the parcel rack next door, sir," the Old Monkey reported.

"This is shameful," said Uncle. "At least twice the number of coaches is needed for decent travelling."

The guard, a shifty, depressed-looking man, came edging along the footboard of the train. He couldn't possibly have walked along the edge of the platform like any normal guard, for the struggling passengers were too tightly packed for that.

"No stop till Number 10. No stop till terminus!"

A howl of rage came from those on the platform and in the train.

"What," Uncle asked the guard sternly, "about those who want to get off?"

The guard said nothing, but pointed to a notice on the station wall opposite the train. It read:

DWARFTOWN RAILWAY

If train becomes overcrowded between stations 1—10 no stops will be made till terminus is reached. Travellers may be set down at required stations on return journey by payment of 10 bananas per stop.

By order.

SIMON EGGMAN (Managing Director)

"This is shameful!" said Uncle, disgustedly.

"Them's my orders," said the guard. At that moment the train started, and the unfortunate guard, still clinging to the outside of the train, was swept into such a narrow tunnel that he had to flatten himself against the carriage. In spite of this a hole was rubbed in the back of his shabby coat, and his skin was beginning to be grazed as the train came to the next station. He did not seem unduly distressed, and went on edging down the train and shouting dismally, but Uncle was horrified.

"This is a disgraceful state of affairs!" he said. "I shall go and see this so-called Managing Director, Eggman, and ask him why he allows such bad working conditions."

"I know where he lives," said Goodman, eagerly. "He's got a big house on Number 10 platform."

"You seem to know more about my castle than I do," said Uncle.

"Well, I get into all sorts of places while I'm looking for rats," said Goodman.

When they got to Number 10 Station they all got out and soon saw the head office, over the door of which was a sign:

DWARFTOWN RAILWAY
Simon Eggman,
Managing Director.
Cheap bananas. Inquire within.

Goodman had as usual darted in front of the party. Now he rushed back to Uncle.

"Oh, sir, if you really want to see what Eggman is like, look in that side window!"

Uncle glanced in the side window and saw a big flabby man sitting in an armchair. Round him were gathered ten fat children, all like him, and all with beady eyes and sharp little teeth. On the table in front of Eggman was a pile of money, and all round the walls were shelves crammed with bananas.

"Another good day!" Eggman was saying. "Trains more crowded than ever, and fares up!"

The children cheered and Eggman tossed them each a banana.

Uncle looked no more, but went round to the office and rang the bell loudly.

In a few moments Eggman appeared. He had put on a thin black silk dressing-gown, and looked very respectable.

"Oh sir," he said in a humble voice, "how good of you to patronize our little railway. Times are hard, and I'm having great difficulty in paying the staff."

Uncle struck the wooden counter a heavy blow with his trunk, a sure sign he was getting angry.

"Listen, Eggman," he said, "I have a number of serious charges to make."

"Charges?" said Eggman, looking shocked and surprised at the same time. He must have been a very good actor.

"Yes, charges," said Uncle gravely. "First, you are running a railway in my castle without my permission. Second, you are running it inefficiently. Third, you are under-paying your employees. Fourth, you are defrauding the public. Answer these charges."

Uncle twisted a stone club in his trunk as he spoke.

Eggman suddenly took an egg out of the pocket of his dressing-gown and threw it at Uncle and then tried to rush out of the door, but in a moment Gubbins had him by the leg. He might as well have struggled with a travelling crane. He was lifted and placed before Uncle who was wiping the egg out of his eyes with a towel handed to him by the One-Armed.

By this time a large number of dwarfs had collected. It was a good moment to pronounce judgment on Eggman, here in front of so many of those who had suffered at his hands. Even Goodman looked grave.

"You are guilty, Eggman," said Uncle in slow and solemn tones. "If any proof were needed your abominable action in throwing that egg at me has stamped you as an enemy of society. This is the sentence."

He paused to let his words sink in.

"First I shall take all your money and bananas—"

At this moment he noticed Hitmouse bristling with skewers and writing busily in a hating book.

"There is a reporter from the *Badfort News* present," he said. "Catch him!"

But the little wretch was too quick. He vanished in the crowd. Uncle knew that he would make the most of the unfinished sentence about money and bananas.

"To continue," said Uncle. "I will take all your money and bananas, Eggman, and start a fund called the Dwarfs' Benevolent Fund."

There were deafening cheers from the crowd.

"And you, Eggman, will work as a porter for those you have so heartlessly robbed, and lastly the railway shall be called the Homeward Railway. I shall appoint a new manager, double the number of coaches, and the train will stop at every station on every journey."

The cheering that followed this announcement went on for more than a quarter of an hour.

Uncle made a fine picture as he stood there, his trunk gently waving to and fro and a benevolent, yet firm look on his face.

But that night a special edition of the *Badfort News* came out.

THE DICTATOR'S BIGGEST STEAL

We have pointed out, again and again, that the Dictator of
Homeward is a thief. This afternoon he publicly admitted
this. Filled with envy at the success of Mr Simon Eggman
who has managed the Dwarftown Railway so well that the
trains are always full, he got one of his brutal followers to
knock Mr Eggman down and then calmly said: "I shall take
all your money and bananas."

When Uncle read this he said in a stern voice: "I shall call at
the office of the *Badfort News* tomorrow."

FIFTEEN

Office of the *Badfort News*

THE next day Uncle got up still determined to go to the office of the *Badfort News*, and see what he could do to reform things. The paper was a disgrace. It was full of attacks against the people of Homeward, and against any sober, honest person or decent trader.

The advertisements were also very low. Burglar outfits were offered for sale, also knuckledusters and false money. Uncle felt it was high time it was stopped.

The Old Monkey knew it was very dangerous for his master to go to Badfort, but nothing would move Uncle from his purpose.

He only took one stone club with him, to use as a walking stick, but he did take Cloutman and Gubbins as companions. This was a great relief to the Old Monkey. Also he was glad to have the cat Goodman with them because he makes even the most dangerous expedition cheerful.

Strangely enough, nobody noticed Uncle and his party walk into Badfort. This must have been because the scob fish were coming up Black Treacle Creek that day.

It is quite an event when this happens, for the Badfort people get scob oil from this small savage fish for their lamps, and also some people eat them.

Now, over by the stream which runs through Badfort, people were fighting and shouting over one small scob fish.

"This place never changes," said Uncle; "it's always full of quarrelling and shouting."

All the same they kept their eyes keenly on the look-out for any attack as they walked across the open space, scattered with tin cans and litter of all sorts, towards a broken-down hut, over the door of which hung a crooked sign which read:

OFFICE. BADFORT NEWS

It seemed to be a disused dance hall. There was no floor, for it had been torn up for firewood long ago. In the muddy earth were many impressions of a large pair of feet. Along one wall ran a daubed message:

THE BADFORT NEWS NOW SELLS THREE
MILLION COPIES PER DAY

Underneath this was a counter, and behind the counter stood Beaver Hateman. He had his back to Uncle, and a man who looked like a commercial traveller was trying to sell him something.

Uncle walked up to the counter and smacked it loudly with his trunk. Hateman threw a can of cold soup over his shoulder on to Uncle's velvet jacket; otherwise he took no notice.

"Attend to me!" shouted Uncle in a voice of thunder.

Hateman still did not look round, but said: "I seem to hear somebody shouting who has a voice nearly as rotten as the Dictator's!"

Uncle was so overcome by this cool, vile behaviour that he stood speechless for a moment.

The salesman lifted a large pair of boots on to the counter.

"These are the Ben Bandit Patent Policeman's Boots, Mr Hateman," he said. "The heels are normal heels as long as the copper is just walking along, but the moment starts to run after a thief they explode. That soon brings him to a standstill."

"How much?" asked Hateman.

"Fifty pounds. It would be a hundred to anybody else."

"All right," said Hateman. "My usual terms. One halfpenny at the end of the first six months, one penny at the end of the year, and so on. Then you've always got some money coming in."

"That's not good enough," said the salesman in a disappointed voice.

"Oh, isn't it?" said Hateman, and seized the boots and pushed them under the counter. "I'm tired of haggling. I'm confiscating the boots for your own good. If the police found you with them you'd be for it. I'm doing you a good turn by taking them."

"But what about paying?"

"Paying! I've confiscated them! Nobody pays for a thing that's confiscated, you moondog! And now get out!"

Hateman seized the salesman and flung him out of a side door into some bushes. Then he slammed the door and turned round, and for the first time looked at Uncle.

"Oh, it's you!" he said. "What d'you want?"

"I've come on serious business," said Uncle, watching him closely and leaning on his stone club.

"You mean you want to subscribe to the *Badfort News!*"

This cheeky remark made Uncle boil over.

"Your rag is vile!" he shouted, and then noticed that Hateman was trying to edge towards an open case of duck bombs. Duck bombs are missiles often used by the Badfort crowd. When they burst they cover the person they hit with a vile sticky juice which stops him moving.

"Hold him, boys!" he shouted.

Cloutman and Gubbins instantly pinned Hateman by the arms.

"Now," said Uncle, "I mean to see the place where you print your degraded rubbish!"

The cat Goodman, who had been prowling round finding out things, came back to Uncle.

"It's here, sir, down this staircase. I can hear the clicking of a printing machine."

"Lead the way," said Uncle. "Bring the scoundrel with you, boys," he added.

Cloutman and Gubbins forced Hateman down a narrow

staircase, and Uncle, the Old Monkey and Goodman followed. In a damp dark room they found a small badger working a rickety old printing machine.

"Are you employed by this man?" asked Uncle, pointing at Hateman.

"Yes, sir," said the badger. "He pays me a saucer of beans a day, and he's going to pay me ten pounds a week when I can set type a bit better."

"*Going* to pay you!" said Uncle in bitter tones. "The old story!"

"Oh, sir," said the Old Monkey, "the poor little chap is actually chained to the machine!"

"Cloutman," said Uncle, "set this unfortunate creature free! Gubbins, hold hard on to your prisoner meanwhile."

It would have done you good to see Cloutman just take the chain and break it as if it were a thread.

"Am I to go, sir?" asked the badger in astonishment.

"Yes, and be quick!" said Uncle.

The small badger was off up the stairs so quickly they couldn't see him move. All they could see was the end of his chain as he whisked up the stairs.

"And now," said Uncle, turning to Hateman, "let us look at the news that unfortunate creature has been setting."

"Oh, shut up!" shouted Hateman, whose face was so full of rage it looked as if it had been roasted. "You've lost me my best printer! He was an apprentice too. His father paid good money for him to learn the printing trade."

"His father," said Uncle, "never thought of him being fastened with a chain!"

"And why not?" said Hateman. "Have you never heard of anyone being bound as an apprentice? I bound him a bit firmer than usual, that's all!"

But Uncle was hardly listening. His eye had been caught by the grimy piece of paper held by a skewer against the printing machine. It was the copy from which the badger had been working.

"Hitmouse!" hissed Goodman. "That's his writing, sir, I'd know it anywhere!"

"This abominable sheet," said Uncle, and breathed heavily, "is the work of your degraded reporter, Hitmouse."

"'The Dictator Hit by Well-aimed Egg!'" read out the Old Monkey in a shocked voice. "Oh, sir!"

Hateman laughed a horrible bubbling laugh. It was too much.

"Gubbins," said Uncle, "is that a sliding door in the wall?"

"Yes, sir," said Gubbins, "it leads to the moat."

"Open it," said Uncle to the Old Monkey.

Helped by Goodman, the Old Monkey managed to slide the door open. Cloutman and Gubbins dared not let go of Hateman who would have been up the stairs in a flash. As it was he struggled and yelled, but could do nothing.

When the door slid back they could see, beyond a slope, the black waters of Badfort moat, thick with old cans and rubbish, a painful contrast to the clear beautiful stream round Uncle's house. Beyond the moat lay the oozy stretches of Gaby's Marsh.

"Very satisfactory," said Uncle, moving back for a run.

"Now look here," said Hateman, "if you kick me up all the things I've done to you so far will seem like rapture."

The Hateman crowd often kick each other, but they hate being kicked up by Uncle. It is ignominious and painful, and Uncle only does it when it is well-deserved.

"Your threats have no effect on me," said Uncle.

"I shall have such a revenge that people will go grey when they hear of it!" yelled Hateman.

"Let him go, boys!" shouted Uncle.

Hateman bounded forward in an effort to get clear away. In vain did he try to dive into some withered bushes. There was a thud, and the body of the odious editor of the *Badfort News* soared up, up, up into the clear blue sky.

Hateman let out a yell so furious that it frightened hundreds of herons who rose squawking and flapping with him.

"Oh, sir, what a beauty!" sighed the Old Monkey. "One of your very best!"

"He's coming down in Gaby's Marsh," said Gubbins, "where the crabs are!"

"And the barking conger eels," said Goodman, running round in circles.

Indeed, as they watched, muddy water rose in chocolate-coloured fountains away in the distance.

"I trust," said Uncle, turning away, "that we have seen the last of those evil writings in the *Badfort News*."

But the Old Monkey shook his head as they began to walk thoughtfully home.

The Sinking Parade

IT WAS the Old Monkey's birthday and he had had a splendid
lot of presents, gum boots (though he doesn't often wear them,
as his legs are too thin), a squash racket, a couple of chestnut
roasters and several other things. His bedroom gets fuller and
fuller. For instance, his window is so surrounded by tins of
corned beef that it's like looking through a tin tunnel.

Uncle wanted to arrange a little extra treat for him.

"Is there anywhere you would like to go for a trip?" he asked.

The Old Monkey's eyes shone. A trip to somewhere new in the
castle is what he loves.

"Oh sir," he said, "d'you remember when we were on our way
to the Fish-Frying Academy we saw a notice 'To the Sinking
Parade'. I've often wondered what it could be."

"We'll go," said Uncle. "Tell the One-Armed to get ready."

The One-Armed was not ready for once. He had been away
gathering chrysanthemums for the Old Monkey's birthday. He
soon appeared, so surrounded by flowers that he looked like a
walking bouquet. The moment he heard of the plan he hurriedly
presented his flowers to the Old Monkey and waddled off to get
his pack.

"I seem to remember the notice was on the top of a battened-down hatchway," said Uncle. "We'd better take Cowgill as there may be some engineering work to be done."

They also took Goodman and Butterskin Mute who had come to see the Old Monkey on his birthday. Cloutman and Gubbins were left to keep guard.

They made their way to the summit of one of Homeward's lofty towers, and there they found, as they expected, a hatchway labelled 'Sinking Parade'.

Cowgill had brought a powerful wrench and they soon had the cover loose. As the work was going on they thought they could hear a lot of shouting, and when, with a united effort, the hatch cover was pulled aside, they saw it had formed the roof of a room.

The members of an indignant family were staring up at them. An old man and woman, a young couple and a number of children.

"Who are you, you great fat bounder in a purple dressing-gown?" yelled the old man.

"Modify your language," said Uncle, sternly.

"Here we are having to double up with Grandpa and Grandma because of the housing shortage," shouted the young woman, shaking her fist, "and the moment we move in the place is broken up by a lot of inquisitive, idle rubber-necks!"

Uncle had had enough of this, so he jumped down and put some money on the table.

"We have come to pay a visit to the Sinking Parade," he said. "If we have, unwittingly, done damage to your roof here is payment. All we want is to be shown the way to the Parade."

The whole family stopped being indignant and stared at the money. They seemed dazed by it. At last the old man, who said

his name was Tom Fullglass, recovered sufficiently to insist that
he should show them the way to the Parade.

He was the worst possible guide. He was very apt to sneeze,
and when he did he sneezed so violently that he turned a somer-
sault. This made him quite uncertain about which way he was
going.

However, he got them into a dark gallery where a lot of people
were sleeping against the walls and said he was sure this was the
right way.

"Who are all these people?" asked Uncle.

Tom Fullglass sneezed again. He turned upside down and
staggered about, and seemed unsure which end of the gallery
they were making for.

"Look here," said Uncle, "I'm losing patience. You are *not* to
sneeze again. It is a very bad habit you've got into. I want a clear
statement about these people. Haven't they got houses to sleep
in?"

Tom Fullglass didn't speak for a bit. He went nearly black in
the face, but managed not to sneeze. Everybody stood around
waiting for him to speak.

"All the houses round here have been grabbed by the Pointer
family. I thought everybody knew that," he said at last.

"I did not know it," said Uncle, "but it is pretty evident from
the sight of these unfortunate people in this gallery that there has
been some monkeying going on. No offence to you, my friend,"
he said, looking at the Old Monkey.

When they got out of the gallery they saw an amazing sight.

Before them was an attractive circular lake with vast towers
grouped round it. Round the lake ran a broad curved walk
labelled Sinking Parade, and on the edge of this walk were a
number of large roomy houses.

Tom Fullglass, now that Uncle's stern eye was not on him, was having an orgy of sneezing, but at last he recovered from this and hurried up to ask if he could guide them further.

Uncle thanked him for his services, paid him half a crown to go away, coupled with a threat of a fine of five shillings if he came back, and most reluctantly he went off, sneezing and turning somersaults, like a living catherine-wheel.

"Let's look at the first of these Pointer houses," said Uncle. It was a fine house, six storeys high. On the door-post was a sign:

MR RICHARD POINTER
No rooms.
No organs.
No circulars.

Mr Richard Pointer was sitting under a cherry tree in his garden dressed in a rather old-fashioned silk suit.

"No rooms!" he shouted as he saw Uncle's party.

Uncle did not reply. He wished to inspect more houses on the Parade before he entered into any discussion.

It was very pretty by the lake. Parties of excursionists kept arriving, and all seemed filled with delight at the great expanse of clear blue water. Some had brought lunch and were already having a meal, sitting on the seats which were liberally scattered around.

Uncle walked further along the Parade. All the houses seemed to belong to the Pointers. One was labelled:

MR FRIENDSHIP POINTER
No rooms.
No organs.
No circulars.
No sellers of eagle beak fish.

Another read:

T. SMIGGS POINTER ESQ.
No rooms.
No organs.
No circulars.
No sellers of eagle beak fish.
No sellers of snout eels.

The largest house, near the middle of the Parade, had a summer-house in front of it. On the gate in gold letters was printed:

MISS JEZEBEL POINTER
No rooms.
No organs.
No circulars.
No sellers of eagle beak fish.
No sellers of snout eels.
No visitors at all unless in possession
of a card which must be examined
by Miss Pointer's personal attendant,
Mr Albert Snell.

"What is all this?" Uncle said irritably. Quite naturally he hates reading notices telling him not to do things when he is in his own house.

He was about to charge up to the summer-house in which Miss Pointer, a rather plain elderly lady, was sitting when something surprising and terrifying happened.

With a loud creaking, as of hidden machinery, a section of the Parade began to sink. It was soon covered with water. Luckily

Uncle and his party were near the gravelled path which rose steeply as it led to Miss Jezebel Pointer's summer-house, but the others on the Parade were soon struggling in the water, and might even have been drowned if two boats with the words 'RESCUE. Price per head, 10s.' printed on their sides had not approached them rapidly. Uncle was appalled to see that before they were admitted to the boat the money had to be handed over.

After this the holiday-makers, wet and frightened, and with their holiday money greatly diminished, were landed on the Parade again.

Before Uncle could get to Miss Pointer a fat man with very short legs ran up to him and said sharply:

"Where's your card? You can't go up there without a card."

Uncle looked him over and then said in a terrifying voice:

"One word more and I'll spill you in the lake."

Snell seemed overpowered and Miss Pointer's face took on a purple hue.

"Who are you?" she asked in a bitter voice. "I don't think I know you."

Uncle lashed himself with his trunk.

"I am Uncle, the owner of this castle, and I don't remember having received any rent from you or any other member of your family."

Uncle could see many wheels and levers in the summer-house, and it seemed clear that it was from here that the whole machinery of the Sinking Parade was controlled. But how?

"There's a small lever there, sir!" whispered Goodman. "I can read the words 'up' and 'down' printed on ivory tablets."

"Where?" asked Uncle.

As he followed Goodman's pointing paw and peered into the summer-house Miss Pointer's hand moved on the lever, and the Sinking Parade began to wobble up and down. Renewed cries came from the holiday-makers who were just beginning to get dry.

"Take your hand from that lever!" roared Uncle, but the Parade went on sinking.

Goodman suddenly leapt through the little window of the summer-house and dashed Miss Pointer's hand from the lever. She screamed but could do nothing.

"Thanks, Goodman," said Uncle.

Then he turned to Miss Pointer.

"A woman as old as you," he said severely, "ought to behave with more dignity and kindness."

"I'm not old," shouted Miss Jezebel angrily. "You ought to see my mother!"

An invalid chair, in which sat a very old woman, was just being wheeled up the path and they all turned to look at it.

"Wheel me right up to the summer-house," the invalid was saying in a surprisingly strong voice. "Working the lever and hearing the waves sloshing and the people shouting is my little daily treat!"

"It's a treat you will have to give up, madam," said Uncle.

"Who is this person?" asked Miss Jezebel's mother, staring at Uncle in a haughty way.

"He says he is the owner of this castle," said Miss Jezebel, sarcastically.

"Nonsense! Snell, turn him out."

Snell twisted his small fat hands together agitatedly.

"I'm afraid, Mrs Pointer," he said, "that he is speaking the truth. I've seen pictures of him."

"Well, I haven't," said Mrs Pointer, "and I don't believe he's the owner of anything."

"You soon will, madam," said Uncle firmly. "From today you and your family will live in one house!"

"One house, impossible!" screamed old Mrs Pointer.

"Your other dwellings will be used to ease the housing shortage in this part of my castle," continued Uncle firmly. "You've had things your own way on this remote tower for far too long. I blame myself for not coming on a tour of inspection before this."

These words so enraged Mrs Pointer that she jumped right out of her invalid chair, seized an iron dog that was used as a doorstop for the summer-house, and hurled it at Uncle.

It missed Uncle and struck a small marble statue of Miss Jezebel Pointer dressed as Mercy and holding two marble children by the hand. It cracked the statue from top to bottom.

"That display," said Uncle, "has quite destroyed your claim to be a helpless invalid. Any person who can sling an iron dog with such energy is not very ill."

"Hear, hear!" said the Old Monkey, his eyes shining with admiration as he gazed at Uncle.

Uncle instructed Cowgill to make the machinery in the summer-house temporarily unusable and went to tell the rest of the Pointers that their houses were about to be taken over for the use of the homeless people in the gallery.

Mr Friendship Pointer said he would rather die on his own

threshold than allow one homeless person to cross it, so Uncle curled his trunk round him and skimmed him like a pebble along the surface of the lake. He bounced five times, and then sank. Then he rose to the surface and started swimming to shore. When last seen he was climbing on to the Parade, a woebegone object.

Uncle made his way back home again in a high state of satisfaction, and the Old Monkey assured him that he had never before enjoyed a birthday so much.

The Sinking Parade is still used, and on many a fine summer afternoon happy bathers enjoy the thrill of being suddenly submerged while they are sitting on benches. This is only done when they are in bathing costumes, and the machinery is under the careful supervision of Cowgill and his engineers.

SEVENTEEN

Little Liz

ONE evening when Uncle was going to bed he heard a sort of shuffling noise at the front door and went to see what it was. Of course he was followed by the Old Monkey who never goes to bed till his master is safely stowed away.

When Uncle opened the door he saw a large bundle hanging from the handle. The handle is about the size of a small pumpkin, for the front door of Homeward is, of course, an elephant's front door, and therefore extremely large.

The bundle, about three feet long, was suspended from the knob by a thick band of leather. Uncle took it down and carried it into the hall. There, under the glare of the golden lamp which burns all night, he saw at once that the bundle contained a living creature of some sort, for movement and muffled sound came from it.

Uncle and the Old Monkey soon had the bundle undone, and saw that it contained a very ugly little girl dressed in a cheap sack dress, and with a handkerchief tied tightly across her mouth. A blue card was pinned to her dress, and she pointed to it, rolling her eyes, while the Old Monkey untied the handkerchief.

This is what the note said:

Dear Kind Sir,

In despair I am leaving my daughter outside your door. A person called Beaver Hateman is trying to kidnap her. If he gets her you know the sort of ransom he will ask for. I could never pay it.

Please, sir, look after my daughter. We call her Little Liz and she is loved by all. She can wash plates and cups, and never breaks more than one at a time.

Will you please shelter her till the danger passes?

Yours in distress,
AMELIA CABLEY

139

"I'm hungry," said Little Liz in rather a rasping voice.

"Give her some milk and a bun," said Uncle.

"One bun is no good to me," said Little Liz. "I said I was hungry."

"I didn't hear the word 'please'," said Uncle frowning. "It is late, and a heavy meal would not be good for you."

While the little girl was wolfing a plate of buns and a quart of milk Uncle took the Old Monkey aside.

"To tell you the truth, I don't much care for the look of this girl," he said. "She reminds me of somebody I don't like—I can't think who."

"Just what I was feeling," said the Old Monkey.

"Well, we can hardly turn her adrift at this time of night. Put

her to sleep in one of those disused pantries off the kitchen where you and Mig can keep an eye on her."

Little Liz went to sleep the moment she lay down on her camp bed. The Old Monkey looked at her for a bit, and then put an extra rug over her and left her.

Whom did she remind him of? He went to bed much puzzled.

Next morning, when the Old Monkey was preparing Uncle's bucket of cocoa, Little Liz bounced into the kitchen shouting:

"Any loin of pork for breakfast, Jacko?"

The Old Monkey flushed. He had never been called Jacko before, and he didn't like it. The girl's manners were really extremely bad. However, he always tried to be kind to little girls, so he said:

"Did you have a good night, my dear?"

"Rotten," she shouted. "I was dreaming about lobsters. What's for breakfast?"

Somehow the Old Monkey controlled himself.

"No loin of pork, anyway," he said. "We have ham and cocoa."

He carried the cocoa-bucket into the hall and the irritating little girl ran after him.

"Ham, goody good!" she screamed. "Who's the cook in this place?"

"Never you mind," said the Old Monkey.

As they got to the hall Uncle came majestically down the stairs, and Goodman folded the morning paper neatly and ran to him with it.

"Oh, what a horrid cat!" said Little Liz. "Keep him away from me."

Uncle put on his great horn-rimmed spectacles, and gave her a look before which even she seemed to wilt a little.

"Take her into her room, lock her in and give her a plain breakfast, and let her stay there till she becomes more polite," he told the Old Monkey. "Gubbins, remove her."

Gubbins had turned up to get his orders for the day, and at the sight of him Little Liz seemed to realize it was useless to rebel. She looked sulky, but she walked meekly with Gubbins to the kitchen.

"Very disagreeable girl, sir," said the Old Monkey. He seldom allows himself to say anything as severe as this.

"I call her detestable," said Uncle.

Goodman, who had run after Little Liz to make sure she wasn't up to anything, now came rushing back.

"Oh, sir," he said, "that's not a proper little girl. I've seen little girls before and they don't look like Little Liz. Don't keep her, sir. Turn her out, sir. There are lots of young rats I like better than her, sir."

Uncle looked at Goodman sternly.

"Now, Goodman," he said, "you mustn't let your worst feelings overcome you. This little girl is in danger from Beaver Hateman. We don't know where Mrs Cabley—that's her mother —lives, and until we do she must stay here."

"I don't believe she's got a mother at all!" said Goodman.

"Goodman," said Uncle even more sternly, "be merciful to the young and helpless. Remember you were once in a similar position and I—"

"*I* wasn't a fraud!" interrupted Goodman beside himself. "*I* didn't try to take you in! You're just being stupid about this girl!"

"Oh, Goodman," said the Old Monkey very shocked, "how can you speak like that?"

"You'd better go and wrap up some parcels," said Uncle, "and cool down."

Goodman went off looking upset and muttering to himself.

Uncle was busy most of the morning with cheques for maize and other correspondence, but towards the end of it the Old Monkey appeared with a twisted-up piece of paper in his hand.

"It's from Little Liz, sir," he said. "She pushed it under her door."

"Let's hope she has taken a turn for the better," said Uncle.

Little Liz had written:

Revered and honourable Uncle,

I am afraid I upset you a little. The word Uncle is like music to my mother and me, and we often speak about you at dark times. Dear good sir, forgive me and let me ask you one favour. Do take me to your museum, and the dear good monkey as well. I have a feeling you don't want me in your castle much, but if you take me to the museum you'll learn where I live and I can go home.

Yours,

LITTLE LIZ

Uncle frowned as he read this.

"I don't much like the tone of this letter," he said. "It's humble enough, and yet there's a kind of cheek running through it. 'You'll learn where I live,' it says. Perhaps her mother works there! But I tell you what, I've never been to the museum. I told Blenkinsop to stock it when I bought the castle, and it's time we went to see it. I must say I look forward to the prospect of getting rid of this girl. She's nothing but a nuisance."

The Old Monkey jumped for joy. Two good things together, an interesting expedition and the hope of saying goodbye to Little Liz.

"Oh, sir, could Goodman come?" he asked. "I'm sure he's sorry for being rude."

"You can ask him," said Uncle. "To tell you the truth, I well understand how he feels, but he went too far."

The Old Monkey returned in a few minutes looking surprised.

"Goodman says thank you, sir, but if Little Liz is going he would rather stay at home."

"What *is* wrong with that cat?" roared Uncle. "So much fuss about a bad-mannered girl! We'll start after an early lunch— *without him!*"

"Very good, sir," said the Old Monkey sadly.

Little Liz behaved very well during lunch and while they were getting ready. She had a notebook in her pocket and said she was going to put down as much as she could about the specimens in the museum.

"I see by the plan that there is a tea-room at the museum," said Uncle, "so we need not take any provisions."

They started off by going into a boot-cupboard just outside the dining-room door. All they had to do was to pull one of the shelves to one side, but it was important to do that with the main door of the cupboard shut. If you left it open the shelf wouldn't move. It was crowded in the boot-cupboard with the door shut, but after a bit of shoving the shelf moved, and in front of them was a small railway siding with a very small train labelled MUSEUM.

They managed to squeeze into the carriage, though Uncle found it a tight fit, and they were wondering how to start it up when, to their surprise, Noddy Ninety appeared, wearing a train-driver's cap.

"Hello, Ninety," said Uncle. "I haven't seen you since the visit to the treasury. Is Oldeboy still going to Dr Lyre's school as I told him to?"

"Yes," said Ninety, "he goes on Tuesdays and Fridays, and he's dyed his hair grey now, silly chap."

"What are you doing here? I thought you worked on the line between Biscuit Tower and Watercress Tower?"

"I go where there's passengers, and the Museum Railway's busy today," said Ninety. "The fare's sixpence, except for you, of course, sir."

Uncle doesn't pay fares in his own castle, so Ninety had nothing to collect. He soon got the engine started.

At the first stop, which was called Rhino Halt, a thin but very happy-looking man came running to the side of the train.

"Got my museum money at last, Ninety!" he said joyfully.

"Sorry, Needler," said Ninety. "We can't take you today. Full up."

Needler burst into loud sobbing.

"After all I've done to save up! Done without lunch for nineteen days, and all to get into the museum!"

"Let him in," said Uncle; "we'll make room."

Needler's no-lunch habit had made him so thin that he slipped into a very small corner of Uncle's carriage.

Little Liz put out her tongue at him, but Uncle saw her and said sternly:

"If you do that again you will be put off at the next station!"

"I'm sorry," said Little Liz very quickly.

"Also, Needler," said Uncle, "I will pay your fare."

He handed sixpence to Ninety.

Needler burst into tears of joy. It really seemed unnatural for a man to cry so much. His tears overflowed his handkerchief and fell on to the floor in a stream.

"Thank you abundantly, sir," he said. "I never thought I would see this day. The cost of living keeps going up so much. But now what joy I've got in front of me! A long lovely walk through all the museum rooms, tea— they do you well at the tea-room for a halfpenny— and then I'll buy some picture postcards and take the rest of the money home, and live like a prince for a week!"

"I'm only glad you've cheered up," said Uncle, who hates crying of any sort.

The next station was Museum Park. As soon as they got out of the train they saw a gigantic sign printed in gold:

Visitors to the Museum and Park are
warned that the sight of so many
marvels can be overwhelming.
We recommend, in case of faintness,
Gleamhound's Smelling Salts for
Attacks by Burglars. 2s. 6d. per bottle.

"Luckily," said Needler, "I have a bottle of the salts with me. I knew I'd need them as I'm so excited before I start. I'll take a sniff right away."

"Wait!" said Uncle, but he was too late.

Needler had taken out a small green bottle, taken a sniff, and immediately fallen down on the platform.

"Oh dear, Mr Needler's been taken ill!" said the Old Monkey, very distressed.

"Nonsense," said Uncle. "Can't you keep it fixed in your mind that Gleamhound's remedies work backwards. Luckily I have with me some Gleamhound's Paralysing Snuff for Bandits. 'Sprinkle a little in the Bandit's face and he falls flat.' It's a first-class tonic."

Uncle sprinkled a little powder from the box on Needler's face. The effect was immediate. He sat up and said:

"What happened?"

Uncle told him.

"Have the sign altered," he said to Ninety. "It's most misleading."

"I don't think it was there yesterday," said Ninety, "but I'll see to it."

Outside the station was a motor-coach filling up with visitors to the museum. It was rather shabby and blotched with mud, and was labelled:

Roundabout Joyous Route to the
Museum. Visit Mud Ghost, Ezra
Lake and Snowstorm Volcano.

The Old Monkey said he would love to see these things, but Uncle was rather suspicious about the motor-coach as he saw in very small letters: *Manager* B. . . . . H.T. . . N. B. . F. . T. underneath the direction notice.

"Who runs this coach?" he asked Ninety.

"I don't know," said Ninety, puzzled. "It wasn't here yesterday. Things seem different today. I can't make it out."

"It does look as though the Hateman crowd are somewhere about, sir," said the Old Monkey.

"I certainly don't like the look of that coach," said Uncle.

"Oh, let's go in the motor-coach!" shouted Little Liz, jumping up and down.

"We'll walk," said Uncle.

EIGHTEEN

Uncle's Museum

WHEN they got outside the station, Museum Avenue stretched before them. It was called an avenue, though it was actually lined not with trees but with colossal elephants. Each was far bigger than Uncle and stood with trunk upraised.

At first it was rather impressive, but Uncle soon got tired of the long double line of elephants. One huge statue of yourself is all right, but to walk along an avenue of more than life-sized figures of yourself makes you feel small and tired.

Also Needler was counting the elephants in a dull tired voice which got on Uncle's nerves.

"Four hundred and sixty-two, four hundred and sixty—"

"What's all that counting for?" asked Uncle crossly.

"To see how many elephants."

"There are five hundred," said Uncle. "It said so on a small notice at the beginning of the avenue. So will you please stop gargling numbers."

At last they came to a man who was sitting at a table by the side of an elephant statue. Over his head was a board with this inscription:

WISDOM SAGE

Counsellor and General Adviser.
Terms moderate if right, and
immoderate if wrong.
(N.B. Any terms are immoderate
if wrong.)

Wisdom Sage was finishing off a good lunch of roast goose and sage-and-onion stuffing.

"Hallo," he shouted as they approached. "You see here goose stuffed with sage" (pointing at his plate), "and you see here" (pointing to himself) " ... Sage stuffed with goose!"

He burst into a peal of laughter.

Uncle hardly smiled. He was tired and wanted to get on.

"That's an old joke, Sage," he said, "but I'd like to sample your boasted wisdom. How far is it to the end of this everlasting row of elephants?"

"Three hundred yards," said Sage promptly.

Uncle was getting angry.

"If that was true," he said, "we could see the Museum from here, and there's no sign of it!"

"Ha, ha!" said Sage. "It took Blenkinsop a long time to think out this illusion scheme. It's one of his best."

"We'll go on," said Uncle. "I suppose you want to be paid for this piece of wisdom."

"Only two-and-sixpence," said Sage. "If I had been wrong I should have charged you five shillings as wrong advice is always expensive."

Uncle tossed Sage half-a-crown which he pocketed before going on with his lunch.

They pushed forward, and after half-a-dozen more elephants there appeared to be a change in the air. There was a pearly grey mist ahead of them. Suddenly this lifted, and there, just across a large green lawn, stood the museum.

They stood still, lost in wonder.

"Blenkinsop has excelled himself," said Uncle at last.

The building was eight-sided, and made of some sort of pink stone. There were blue arches and high green pinnacles, and the front doorway was stupendous, being built of three pink rocks each as big as a house, and shining with silver stars. In spite of being so very solid, it appeared to change as you looked at it. Sometimes the pink stone turned almost green; sometimes the towers became round instead of square.

As they stood watching a tall red tower that seemed to be turning into a colossal palm-tree, Wisdom Sage came up behind them.

"I forgot to give you one opinion," he said, "but I'll give it to you now. That girl with you, d'you know what she is? She's not a girl but a snake, and that's such a very right opinion that I'll charge you nothing for it."

And he vanished into some flowering bushes.

"I don't like that man," said Little Liz, "and I'll go after him and tell him so."

"If you go back you stay back," said Uncle.

When they got to the museum entrance they found in the hall a large statue of Uncle playing the bass viol.

Underneath it were these words:

OUR FOUNDER—PATRON OF THE ARTS

Uncle was rather gratified by this, and began to hum one of the tunes he played.

"I must ring up the Maestro," he said to the Old Monkey. "It's time I had another music lesson. I've been rather pressed for time recently."

"Oh yes do, sir," said the Old Monkey, who loves going to Watercress Tower where Uncle's music master lives with his friend the Little Lion.

Little Liz giggled behind them.

Uncle turned sharply for he hates being laughed at, but the horrid girl seemed to be looking at a stuffed swordfish hanging on the wall.

"Look at that fish!" she said. "Isn't it lovely? Oh, how I'd like to see that sharp sword go right into Wisdom Sage!"

"You are a very cruel girl!" said Uncle, and determined to get rid of Little Liz the moment they got home. Meanwhile the thing to do was to forget her as much as possible. He bought a Museum Guide, and then, seeing Needler's eager look, bought another for him.

"For me, sir?" said Needler, his eyes filling with tears.

"Yes, and don't cry!" said Uncle.

"Just let me say this—" began Needler.

"Now, look, we haven't time for all that," said Uncle.

"Magnificent — lavish — noble — astonishing— glorious — gift!" said Needler. He spoke so fast it sounded like one long word. This was clearly the day of his life.

Now they all started to look at the exhibits. It was clear that they were in a very fine museum.

Besides having a Natural History section with stuffed animals in it, there was a zoo with living animals.

Here again Blenkinsop had shown great skill. The animals were always near, and always awake. Uncle had a few cakes in his pocket, and he handed them to his party to give to the animals. Little Liz, of course, ate her portion herself.

In the Museum Guide was written:

To do honour to the Founder's well-known kindness to animals, no living creatures are kept in this zoo for more than one day. They are then dismissed to their haunts with three days' ration of choice food. Places in the Museum Zoo are much coveted and there is always a long waiting list of animals ranging from bison to wombats.

"Very gratifying, very gratifying indeed," said Uncle.

Needler had already got his handkerchief out, but seeing Uncle looking at him hastily put it away again.

They then came to a set of rooms devoted to tableaux of the Founder's Life. The first of these showed Uncle as a young, hard-up elephant. Then came his first stroke of fortune and rise to wealth and power. No hint of the regrettable bicycle-stealing incident of his youth.

It was very touching. Uncle forgave Needler's sobs of admiration.

After this they came to a room labelled:

PUBLIC ENEMIES

They were about to go in when Wisdom Sage appeared from the tea-room.

"Just another bit of free advice," he said. "Note, I say *free*. Be careful when you go in there. There is no charge for this, so take good heed of what I say. Keep your eyes open!"

"Oh do be careful, sir!" begged the Old Monkey.

On the door was a tablet.

We give here a representation of a horde of repulsive beings who have long infested this neighbourhood. By the illustrious efforts of the Founder their evil doings have generally been foiled, and the people and animals in this area live in peace and prosperity.

Uncle flung the door open.

Inside, on a low platform, stood a waxwork group showing Beaver Hateman and some of his allies. Filljug and Nailrod were a bit shadowy at the back but Hateman, well to the front, dressed in his worst sack suit and holding a duck bomb ready to throw, really looked very life-like.

With Sage's warning still in his ears, Uncle only took one look and then dropped to the ground.

It was lucky he did so, for the waxwork figure came to life and Beaver Hateman cast the duck bomb at Uncle, using immense force. At the same moment Uncle felt a sharp pain in his leg as Little Liz stuck a skewer into it.

Now the hideous plot was clear. Little Liz had used Uncle's well-known kindness of heart to lure him to the museum.

"Oh, sir, Little Liz is Hitmouse!" shouted the Old Monkey. "Look out, sir! Look out!"

"Oh, infamy!" sobbed Needler, tears spouting from his eyes.

Trumpeting with rage Uncle charged forward, but the danger was over. Seeing that his duck bomb had missed, and had only splashed harmlessly against the passage wall, Beaver Hateman gave an appalling shriek of baffled fury and disappeared down a trapdoor in the floor of the case, and Hitmouse, well, the last they saw of that detestable so-called little girl was the hem of a sack dress vanishing down a ventilator.

Fortunately Uncle was hardly hurt at all. He had a few skewer stabs, but some Magic Ointment, skilfully applied by the Old Monkey, soon put them right.

Needler hung his handkerchief to dry out of a near-by open window. He had been crying so much that his eyes had nearly disappeared.

"Is the danger really past, sir?" he asked. "I've hardly any tears left."

"Good, you won't need any. All is well," said Uncle, once more erect and masterful as he turned to Sage.

"Well, Sage," he said, "your wisdom has saved us from great harm."

He pulled a bag of gold out of his pocket, for although he usually doesn't carry much money he had brought some that day to pay for teas, etc.

"Oh, I don't want anything," said Sage. "I was so very right I can't make any charge."

"Then," said Uncle, "you will please accept this as a token of our great gratitude."

"Very well," replied Sage, "if you put it that way. Goose is dear, and my income is not large. I'm so frequently right."

"And now," said Uncle, "let's go to the tea-room, and have the very best tea they've got."

They soon found the tea-room, an excellent place partly below the museum and looking out on a sunken garden.

The garden kept changing. Some of the roses changed slowly from red to yellow, and some of the bigger flowers actually seemed to come forward and look through the window. In the middle of the lawn was a fountain which sent up a great column of water that curved into a beautiful water-arch. This was big enough to walk under. Now and then pale blue-and-white clouds floated through the garden.

Nine black bears brought in the tea. There were some cakes that almost overpowered you, they were so rich and scented.

While they ate they looked at the postcards Needler had bought. There were two of the outside of the museum and a very good one of the statue of Uncle playing the bass viol.

"Get a couple of those on the way out," said Uncle to the Old Monkey. "I'd like to send one to my aunt, Miss Maidy, and also one to the Maestro."

"Shall I bring you some Blenkinsop Buns?" asked one of the bears when they had been eating for a time. "They're the best of all."

"By all means," said Uncle. "Let's try them."

Blenkinsop Buns looked like ordinary currant buns, but their taste kept changing. One moment they tasted like raspberry jam, the next like honey, and then like banana ice-cream.

"Oh, sir, can I take a Blenkinsop Bun home to Goodman?" asked the Old Monkey. "He's missed so much by not coming to the museum."

"Take one certainly," said Uncle. "In a way we owe the cat an apology. He was quite right to be so suspicious. To think we were giving shelter to the detestable Hitmouse."

"The disguise was very cunning, sir," said the Old Monkey, "but we must be more careful in future."

NINETEEN

The Great Sale

THE sale of bananas and coconuts in aid of aged and distressed badgers which, you'll remember, Uncle had been asked to open, was about to take place.

The King of the Badgers was organizing it, and it looked as if everybody was giving something, and thousands of people were coming.

Truckloads of bananas and coconuts came in every day. Great traction engines pulling trailers loaded with Whang Eggs, a sort of preserved egg painted red specially loved by aged badgers, arrived almost hourly.

Six motor-coaches had been ordered for the day to bring people from Wolftown. Ivan Koff had postponed a meeting of the Dog-Washers' League, so that he might give a vote of thanks to Uncle.

Even doubtful characters like Sir Ben Bandit, the financier, Abdullah the Clothes-Peg Merchant and Mother Jones (from Jones's siding) had sent gifts and promised to come.

The day before the sale the King of the Badgers came to see Uncle to make final arrangements.

"A surprising letter in the post this morning," he said. "Beaver Hateman and all his supporters have written to say they intend to come to the sale, and whatever you, my dear sir, decide to give, they will give more."

"A good statement," said Uncle, "if we can believe it."

"I know you have not yet said what your gift will be, but if you do now perhaps sheer pride will drive this somewhat shifty character to make a great effort to exceed it."

"I warn you," said Uncle, "that Beaver Hateman will think nothing of promising a million crates of bananas and then declaring himself bankrupt."

"Too true, I'm afraid," said the King sadly.

"Therefore," said Uncle, "I see no reason to alter my original plan, and that is to declare what I am going to give on the day. It will be a great surprise, I assure you."

"Oh, I'm certain of that," said the King. "We must just try to be patient."

The sale was to be held in the Badgertown Stadium. A great field had been walled in and thousands of seats had been built round it in tiers. The platform for the opening had been built out a little way into the amphitheatre, and raised so that all who were on it were in full view. There was a table in front of Uncle's chair with a microphone on it. Uncle does not need a microphone of course, his voice of thunder can reach the limit of any building.

The working committee, under the supervision of the King himself, had piled round the platform a positive mountain of bananas, coconuts and Whang Eggs.

When the great day came Uncle put on his best purple dressing-gown, his elephant boots with diamond tips, and a gold hat embroidered with rubies. He also carried his festival watch, a great time-piece almost like a small clock and so covered with jewels that it was hard to see the hands. A special gold-plated traction engine had also been brought out to take him to the stadium.

What a day it promised to be! The sky was blue, the air soft and mild, and as the morning went on files of creatures could be seen crossing the plain on their way to the sale. Even grizzly bears were coming from the mountains, and carrying coconuts too.

After lunch a big crowd of Uncle's followers gathered for the ride to the stadium. There was no need to leave a strong party behind to guard Homeward as Beaver Hateman and his party were actually seen setting out for the sale in old carts, sledges and on broken-down motor-bikes.

Goodman, looking through the field-glasses, reported that he thought they were all there, Beaver Hateman, Hitmouse, Jelly-tussle, Nailrod, and Filljug, to name only a few.

"And Beaver Hateman's got on what looks like a better suit than usual," said Goodman.

"Good," said Uncle. "Let us hope that for once their black hearts have been touched!"

They had a good ride to the stadium. The traction engine was burning sandalwood, and made the air fragrant as they rode along.

Bells rang and trumpets sounded a loud fanfare as Uncle entered the stadium. The King of the Badgers led the way to the platform where a huge chair had been provided for Uncle, and a small gilded throne for himself.

A number of aged and worthy badgers were placed on either side of Uncle, and the Old Monkey and Goodman were given seats near him to represent the many inhabitants of Homeward.

As the procession of dignitaries mounted the platform the Bad-fort crowd entered to take seats near it. They looked almost respectable for once. Beaver Hateman was wearing a new sack suit made out of a potato-bag. There was not a skewer to be seen about Hitmouse, Jellytussle was shaking quietly but far less objectionably than usual, and the ghost Hootman slid in a polite shadowy way into a seat.

Before the ceremony began a hundred young badgers sang a melody: "Hail to Glorious Uncle."

It went well, too, though Beaver Hateman was seen to stop his ears, and Nailrod Hateman sneezed all the time.

The King of the Badgers then spoke:

"Ladies and Gentlemen," he said, "it does me good to see such a vast gathering. Friends from near at hand, and wolves, tigers and bears from remote forests. I am particularly glad, too, to see our hardy adventurous neighbours from Badfort."

At this moment Beaver Hateman's followers broke into their tribal cheer, a deafening yell of "Stinggoon! Stinggoon!"

When he could make himself heard again the King continued:

"But I am sure I voice all your feelings when I say that the most glorious feature of this assembly today is the presence of the much-loved owner of Homeward Castle—"

There was tremendous cheering. To Uncle's surprise Beaver Hateman kept quiet, only stopping up his ears and squinting.

When Uncle rose to speak there was deafening applause that lasted for nearly ten minutes.

"Your Majesty, friends and neighbours," he began. "I think I can say that I am always in sympathy with those who are less fortunate than myself."

Uncle was so sure that Hateman would object that he stopped and looked at him, but Hateman merely sniffed loudly.

"I'm glad this great effort is being made," Uncle went on. "Many need this help. Great quantities of bananas, coconuts and Whang Eggs have been given, and now, my friends, buy and give all you can. I now come to my own personal contribution."

There was dead silence in the stadium. Even the Badfort crowd stopped shuffling, sneezing and sniffing.

Uncle put his hand in his pocket and took out one banana, one coconut and one Whang Egg.

"These are what I mean to give," he said.

There was a moment of shocked silence, and then Hateman yelled:

"A rotten beggarly gift and from the richest man here! I was going to give a million bananas myself, but now I'll give nothing, and I'll show what I think by clearing out now! Give them a joberry, boys!"

Hateman's followers all filed out, singing a hideous song, rattling sticks, and snatching bananas from the pile at the base of the platform.

When they had gone Uncle continued:

"I will now finish the sentence I began before I was interrupted. At all times I wish to avoid the appearance of display, so I began my speech very quietly. I repeat: my gift will be *one* banana, *one* coconut, and *one* Whang Egg—" he paused impressively— "for every minute of the next five years. Some of you who are good at arithmetic can work out what that means!"

The badgers are not good at arithmetic, but they knew this meant a vast number, and their applause was deafening.

While the cheering was going on the King of the Badgers motioned to his court mathematician, Professor Badgerinstein, and had a whispered exchange with him.

As soon as the cheering stopped the King said:

"Professor Badgerinstein has gone to feed the figures into the court computer. We now await the results of the calculations. Meanwhile, I can safely say that all sick and aged badgers will be splendidly looked after for years to come. Now one more cheer for our benefactor—"

Uncle gave one smile round, waved his trunk, and took his seat, perhaps a trifle heavily, in the huge chair provided for him.

Then tragedy struck.

There was a sudden appalling crash and Uncle, his chair, and

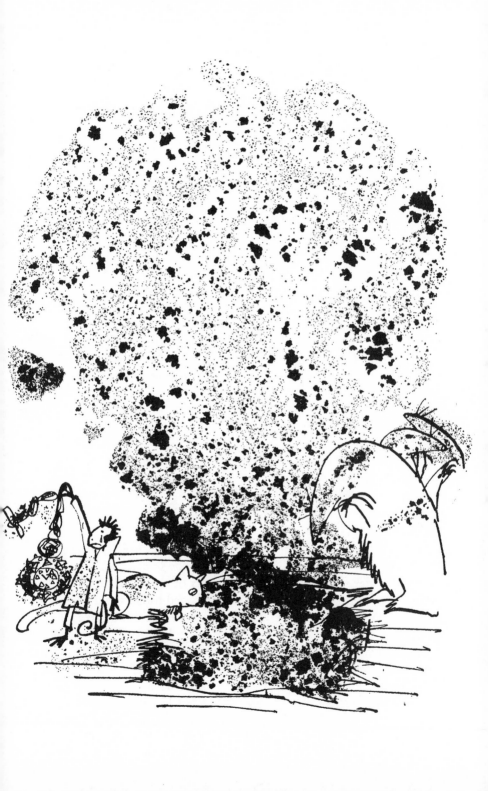

his table disappeared together into the hollow place beneath the platform. For a moment everybody was struck dumb. Then a great cloud of dust rose and obscured the platform. This was no ordinary dust. It seemed to have pepper in it, and everybody was taken with violent sneezing.

Even while sneezing, the Old Monkey and Goodman managed to crawl to the edge of the jagged hole and peer into it.

But there was nothing to see—even when the dust subsided. Uncle had disappeared. So had his table and chair, and the piece of platform on which he had stood. All that was left of his splendid presence was the great jewelled festival watch which must have had fallen from him as the platform gave way. The Old Monkey gathered it up, weeping.

"It was sawn through. The platform was sawn nearly through!" said Goodman. "Look, look!"

Goodman and the Old Monkey examined the broken edge of wood, and while they were doing so Badgertown police arrived and confirmed their suspicions. The whole square of platform on which Uncle's chair had been placed needed only the extra pressure given by Uncle as he sat down after his speech to collapse entirely.

Loud wailing arose, and everywhere groups of melancholy badgers began searching for their benefactor.

Darkness was coming on, and the Old Monkey was distracted. There seemed no clue, no hope.

All at once there was a clatter of hooves, and a lean man wearing a cowboy hat rode up on a sweating horse. He was called Wolfskin Webber and lived near Badfort on the Wolftown side.

"You lookin' fer der big guy?" he shouted.

"Yes, yes," came from a thousand anxious voices.

"Wal, I jest cam' ridin' pas' Badfort, and I see a lot o' dem

Hateman guys with a big furniture van. They was laffin' fit ter split."

"Go on, go on," gasped the Old Monkey. "Did you see inside the van?"

"Nope, I never," said Wolfskin Webber, "I don't hang aroun' dem guys no more n' I kin help, but I hear a sorter trumpetin' and buttin'—"

This was it. The terrible secret was out. A council of war was held at once with the Old Monkey acting as chairman. It was clear now that a furniture van with a sliding open top had been backed in below the platform, and that when the floor had given way Uncle had been dropped neatly in, and had at once been motored off to Badfort. And while this was being done the rest of the Badfort crowd had thrown pepper in the air to confuse his friends and make a quick getaway possible.

The position was indeed grave.

"Back to Homeward," said Captain Walrus, "to collect stone clubs and other fighting materials—and then make a united attack on Badfort."

The meeting agreed that this was the best thing to do.

"But it will take time!" said the Old Monkey. "I can't wait. He may be very stunned and tortured. I must go and do what I can!"

"I'll come with you," said Goodman.

Captain Walrus and Cowgill promised to get things quickly organized at Homeward, and the Old Monkey and Goodman started for Badfort. They knew they were going into terrible danger but they had to do it.

"Luckily I've got my savings in a money-bag under my shirt," said the Old Monkey. "I often carry it with me in case of need."

"That gives me an idea," said Goodman. "Today's Tuesday, and Blenkinsop has a branch at Sable Gulf that is open from six to six-thirty. We might just catch him. Let's see if he can think of anything."

"He'll take too long," said the Old Monkey miserably. "You remember the short cut to the dwarfs' drinking fountains!"

"You never know," said Goodman. "As it's urgent he might hurry for once!"

They were pleased to see a light still burning in Blenkinsop's small wooden hut in Sable Gulf. Not far beyond towered the vast, black bulk of Badfort.

Luckily the wizard had stayed late, for people had been so occupied with the sale that he knew that any customers needing spells would only come after it was over.

"Wizard," panted the Old Monkey, desperately, "I need your help—now quickly!"

The Old Monkey was so out of breath—he isn't as used to running as Goodman is—that Goodman had to tell the tale of the kidnapping.

"I'll help, of course," said Blenkinsop. "Wait a minute while I get a kangle-pot and a bit of moon-misty flamingo, and—"

"Please, please, Mr Blenkinsop," pleaded the Old Monkey. "I can't wait while you do a spell, I can't!"

"I can't promise results without a spell," said Blenkinsop.

"What about Clutchclamp?" said Goodman.

"What d'you know about Clutchclamp?" said Blenkinsop crossly.

"I signed for the registered parcel at Wizard Glen when you bought some," said Goodman. "I remember what a fuss you made about it being so valuable and putting it in the safe at once. And I—"

"What is Clutchclamp?" interrupted the Old Monkey. "Do hurry!"

"Clutchclamp! That's a good idea," said Blenkinsop, "and I have a small quantity here. But it won't do. It costs too much!"

"*Give* it to us," said Goodman. "Surely you can do that for once! For Uncle. Come on, give it to us—free!"

"If you knew anything about wizard work," said Blenkinsop, "you'd know Clutchclamp won't work unless paid for *in cash*!"

"Prove it!" cried Goodman excitedly. "Prove it! Go on. Can't you see the situation's desperate? Give it us now! I always remember how mean you were over saucers of milk and the way you—"

"*I* can pay for Clutchclamp, whatever it is—now," said the Old Monkey.

"I doubt it," said Blenkinsop. "It is a rare pill which makes the person who swallows it invisible. It also opens locked doors. And—it costs exactly one hundred pounds!"

"I have a hundred pounds four shillings and sixpence," almost shouted the Old Monkey, fumbling for his well-worn wallet, "all my savings—here."

"Who'd have thought it!" said Blenkinsop.

"*You'd* never give all your savings to help *any*body—that I do know!" cried Goodman.

"You'd better be more polite or I'll put a spell on you!" Blenkinsop warned him.

Blenkinsop went to a small safe and brought out a round green box in which lay one bright pink pill.

"Swallow that," Blenkinsop told the Old Monkey. "It will last for twenty-four hours."

The Old Monkey swallowed the pill, and sent Goodman to Homeward to say what he had done, and to urge them to hurry with preparations for the attack.

The Old Monkey, feeling very frightened, for he was still not

sure if the pill would work, walked up to the front gate of Bad-fort. A sentry was there, sitting on a barrel with a crossbow by his side, but as the Old Monkey went past him he only moved slightly to take another banana from a pile in front of him.

The Old Monkey felt better. He really was invisible.

In the big front hall of Badfort a monster meeting was being held, presided over by Beaver Hateman. The Old Monkey paused by the open door to listen.

Sigismund Hateman was singing a song with a chorus of "Stinggoon" which everybody yelled.

> "See that pompous humbug Unc
> On the platform raise his trunk,"

sang Sigismund, and the rest all shouted: "Stinggoon! Stinggoon! STINGGOON!"

> "Watch him spouting like a pump,
> Watch him *sit*, the oily lump:
> That's the moment—
> CRUMP!
> CRUMP!
> CRUMP!"

At every 'CRUMP' they stamped their feet; then they burst again into the chorus:

> "Stinggoon! Stinggoon! STINGGOON!"

The Old Monkey felt shaken. Although he was invisible the loud singing and rhythmic stamping frightened him.

"We'll have a million out of the old dog as the lowest ransom!" bellowed Beaver Hateman. He threw a Black Tom bottle out of the door, just missing the Old Monkey. It struck the sentry, and stunned him.

"So much the better for us when the attack begins!" thought the Old Monkey, shuddering as he hurried on.

He did not know where to go in the rickety galleries of Badfort. There were hundreds of rooms, many with the roofs falling in, and all the passages were piled with rubble and broken glass. The only light was an occasional gleam from a scob-oil lamp.

He dared not call Uncle's name for fear the party below might hear. What could he do?

He was just standing at the door of a miserable room labelled 'Burglar's Outfits' and feeling hopeless, when he remembered what Blenkinsop had said about Clutchclamp.

"It will make you invisible and open doors."

"I'll trust to the magic," thought the Old Monkey, and felt a sudden urge to turn round and go back. He returned nearly to the entrance. In the corner there was a big stone staircase he had not noticed before, and his feet seemed to go up the broken dirty steps without any effort.

At the top of the steps there was a huge door fastened with a chain and a big lock, and before he could even use his magic power and go through it he heard a firm voice beyond it saying:

"I'll never pay that scoundrel a ransom of a million pounds! No, I will not, even if I stay here all my life!"

The Old Monkey's heart was filled with delight. He had found Uncle.

TWENTY

The Rescue

As HE looked at the massive iron-bound door the Old Monkey repeated to himself as bravely as he could: "That door will open."

To his unspeakable joy the door began to open slowly and softly. No rattling of chains.

Uncle did not see it move for he was peering out of a small barred window.

"Sir!" whispered the Old Monkey.

Uncle turned and saw the open door. Nobody was there. Nobody. Was this a trick?

He stood there watchful, wondering.

"I'm here to help you, sir," whispered the Old Monkey.

"Where are you?" asked Uncle, looking in the air, everywhere. "I can't see you!"

"Shush, sir! Don't speak so loudly. I'm invisible because of Blenkinsop's spell! I *am* here, really, sir, right here in the doorway—" The story poured out of him. He was so excited he could hardly keep his voice in a whisper.

When Uncle had heard him through, the old ring came back into his voice, his eyes flashed. He was feeling himself again.

"You have done magnificently," he said, "and I shan't forget it! Now let's take a look at these gentry downstairs. You say a strong party is on the way from Homeward?"

"Yes, sir."

"If only I had a stone club or two!"

They crept down the stairs. At the bottom was a recess.

"Look, sir!" whispered the Old Monkey.

There were two weighty objects fastened to the wall, and written underneath them were the words:

These stone clubs were captured from the Dictator
of Homeward by B. Hateman Esq., M.A., and are placed
here as trophies of his skill.

"That's better!" said Uncle, pulling them from the wall.

"Excuse me, sir," said the Old Monkey, "I've still got the power of the spell in me, and we're passing over a trapdoor. I can see through it and directly below are two great underground vats filled with Black Tan and Leper Jack."

"Open the trapdoor," said Uncle, "and prop it open with stones."

It was easy enough to do this as there are always lots of stones scattered about in Badfort. The singing and shouting were loud now, and soon they stood in the doorway of the celebration room.

Beaver Hateman, at the head of the long stone table, had just risen, smiling hideously, to speak.

"Well, lads," he said. "This is the best day's work we've ever done. We've got the Dictator safe at last—twenty rescue parties can't get him out of that upstairs room! Let's visit him and tell him the ransom terms. That'll make him suffer!"

"Can I stick a skewer into him, sir?" said Hitmouse. "I've made a big one!"

"Of course, of course, and see a strong article about the meanness of millionaires goes into the *Badfort News* tomorrow. Come on, boys!"

"Stinggoon!" came the harsh, sonorous chorus as everybody rose.

At that moment Beaver Hateman saw Uncle. He seemed, hardened as he was, to turn to stone.

As he stood staring at the massive figure, holding the two clubs there was a clatter of many feet outside, and above that sound the voice of Captain Walrus could be heard raised in true sea-dog thunder.

"Steady! Keep your eyes lifted for the swabs. Marlinspikes ready!"

Beaver Hateman dived under the table and slithered past Uncle's legs like a maddened snake.

But Uncle turned just in time. Beaver Hateman made straight for the open space in the centre of Badfort. Uncle knew well that he planned to get lost in the maze of rooms which surrounded it. This he was determined to prevent.

Uncle thundered after him, and caught him just as he was getting near the office of the *Badfort News* on the other side of the square.

Even for Uncle it was a great kick-up.

Beaver Hateman was holding a huge lighted cigar in his hand, and the wind made it glow so that everybody could see in the sky what looked like a slowly soaring red light.

Then it came down, down, down, towards Gaby's Marsh.

In the meantime Captain Walrus and his party were driving the rest of the Badfort crowd before them with blow after blow. Some managed to escape into the rickety galleries, but most were forced into the same marsh, filled with barking conger eels and biting crabs, in which their leader lay engulfed.

And Uncle had not finished yet. He seized a scob-oil lamp and flung it through the open trapdoor into the underground tank filled with Leper Jack.

"Everybody get out!" shouted Uncle to his party.

At once, in the entrance to Badfort, a great eruption took place. The liquids stored in the vats were fearfully inflammable, and one set fire to the other. The flames mounted into a ghastly fountain of purple fire. This lit the countryside for many miles,

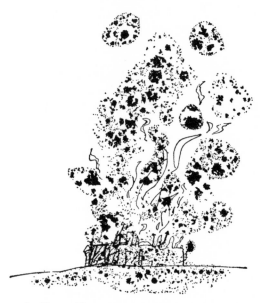

and all Badfort seemed turned into a leaping mass of sinister flame.

Uncle and his party stood for a minute or two watching, and then Uncle said:

"We will now quietly and joyfully march home, our pathway lit by the destruction of the vilest castle of infamy ever constructed."

In the hall of Homeward Uncle suggested they had a short festive supper and then went to bed. It seemed funny to see a flagon of hot cocoa apparently approaching Uncle by itself, for the Old Monkey was still invisible, of course. He played a very good trick on Goodman, going into a corner and squeaking like a rat. You should have seen the way Goodman dashed to catch a rat that wasn't there! Everybody laughed very much, and so did Goodman.

"As for tomorrow," said Uncle, "we will have a quiet day of festive congratulation by ourselves, when the Old Monkey, and all of you, will be suitably rewarded."

"But everybody will want to come, sir," said Captain Walrus.

"If they like to come we can't stop them," said Uncle, "but no public festival is to be arranged."

But they all knew nothing could stop the next day being observed as a day of revelling.

Uncle was soon in bed and snoring happily, but Cowgill said to Captain Walrus:

"I say, old chap, don't you think we'd better have a few illuminations and flags for tomorrow night? It won't take long to arrange."

"I agree with you," said the Captain, "and I've got a special electric star in my lighthouse that I've been wanting to try out for months."

So they all went to bed, after a last glance out of the window to see if Badford was still burning. It was, though not as violently as it had been.

Next morning, when Uncle awoke, the Old Monkey was already by his bedside. The spell had now worn off and Uncle smiled when he saw him.

"Ah, nice to see you again, my friend," he said. "You look none the worse for your terrible experiences, I'm glad to say."

"Neither do you, sir," said the Old Monkey. "The King of the Badgers is already here with an illuminated address for you."

"I said no public rejoicing," said Uncle, "but it's well meant. Show him in."

The King of the Badgers had already had breakfast, but he joined Uncle in a golden flagon of cocoa.

He told Uncle it would be impossible to prevent crowds of people from coming to congratulate him personally.

"Well," said Uncle, "I shall see they are well provisioned, but my chief purpose today is to make a presentation to the Old Monkey."

After the king had gone Uncle and the Old Monkey had a look through the telescope at Badfort. The volcano of flame had pretty well burnt itself out, but Badfort, although even more battered than before, was still standing. The fact is it's not very inflammable, as nearly all the doors and windows have been used for firewood.

"It can't be helped," said Uncle. "At any rate they have had a terrific lesson."

By the evening many thousands of visitors had arrived and it seemed impossible to avoid some sort of public ceremony.

Uncle and the Old Monkey sat side by side on a marble bench supported by six stone lions, and after a few words of congratulation from the King Uncle spoke.

"Friends," he said, "it is always encouraging when skilfully laid schemes of crime come to nothing, and you have all been rejoicing with me in a mighty and glorious victory. I greatly value the many unexpected gifts that have been sent to me. It is hard to single out any when all have been so good, but I was greatly touched when your revered monarch brought from his private art gallery a hitherto unknown picture of myself opening the dwarfs' drinking fountains. It is by the great artist Waldovenison Smeare, and, as you know, his works are practically priceless.

"I thank you all for your kind thoughts. Most of all I thank all my supporters for their prompt and brave support last night. Under the leadership of Captain Walrus, you all, Cowgill, Cloutman and Gubbins, Mig, Butterskin Mute, and Whitebeard, formed a strong attacking party. Goodman the cat used his knowledge of spells to get Wizard Blenkinsop to act swiftly. Mr Will Shudder and Mr Benskin held the fort here. All behaved nobly, and I thank you, but my chief desire today is to give special honour to my faithful friend, the Old Monkey. Last night he outdid all his previous achievements. Alone he made his way to Badfort, after spending the whole of his life savings in the purchase of one powerful spell with which he succeeded in liberating me!"

Here the applause became deafening.

"He put down one hundred pounds to save me. All he had. I now take this bag containing one thousand gold pieces and hand it to him."

Screams of delight greeted this.

"All I have left to say," continued Uncle, "is that I would give my friend far more, but he has scarcely room to stow it. I will merely say he can always count on me to the full resources of my fortune."

Uncle seized the Old Monkey in his trunk, and, holding him high above the crowd, said:

"Three cheers for the most faithful friend in the world!"

As Uncle put the Old Monkey gently down again the King of the Badgers came forward with a glittering medal attached to a broad golden ribbon.

"The King of the Badgers," Uncle announced, "wishes to bestow on the Old Monkey the highest honour in his kingdom. Our friend now becomes a Knight of Bustard Land!"

The order was bestowed, and the cheering began again. As it was at last dying down Uncle held up his trunk for silence.

"And now, my friends," he said, "I want you to spend the rest of the evening in rejoicing. Cowgill, please turn on the illuminations."

Uncle had hardly stopped speaking before everywhere shone out in blue, red, silver, green and yellow light, and high, high, above Lion Tower, on the edge of which Walrus Tower stands like a pencil, shone Captain Walrus's tremendous new star.

The revelry was in full swing when a young badger brought Uncle a letter that had just been handed in at the gate.

It was from Beaver Hateman and read as follows:

> To the Dictator and Swindler
>
> So you got away last night did you, you oily bounder? Just like you to set our noble mansion on fire, but I'll tell you, you firebug, that you did us a good turn. All the money-lenders' offices have been burnt out. We owed a lot to these gentry, but now all the books and I.O.U.s are burnt and we are free of debt!
>
> I said we would get a lot out of you and we have.
>
> We are at once starting a revenge so fearful that anyone who speaks of it will develop lockjaw.
>
> B.H.

"That fellow takes some putting down, I must say," said Uncle. "He'd get out of anything."

The Old Monkey was looking through the telescope at Badfort.

"They've got out some broken chairs and made a little fire. I think I can hear faint singing, sir. They seem to be having some sort of party."

"Party!" said Uncle in disgust. "Come, let's forget them and have a good sleep and then a few days of congratulation and comfort."

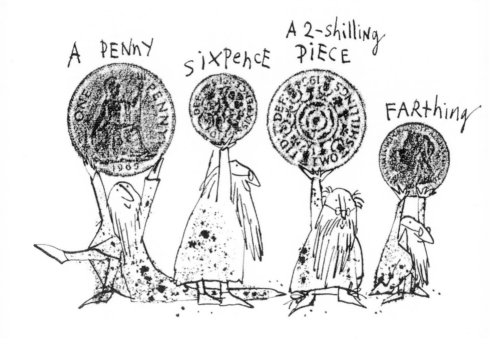

A PENNY   SIXPENCE   A 2-shilling PIECE   FARthing

Uncle's Money

In Uncle's country they use pounds, shillings and pence. As the Old Monkey does Uncle's accounts, we asked him what these were worth in U.S. money.

"A *farthing*," he said, "is so small that it's only used nowadays by the dwarfs. It's worth the fourth of a penny."

"How much is a *penny*?"

"Oh, sir, that's easy! A *cent* — you also call a cent a penny! Then twelve pennies make a shilling."

"Twelve pennies? So a *shilling*'s rather more than a *dime*?"

"That's right, sir. And a two-bob piece — I mean, a *two-shilling* piece — is rather more than a *quarter*. Then, of course, twenty shillings make a pound — "

"Of course? How much is a *pound* worth? Let's see — about *three dollars*

"Very roughly. And I always reckon, sir, that a million pounds is worth about three million dollars." The Old Monkey added: "Very roughly."

"But what about these others — half-crowns, guineas?"

"Half-a-crown is two shillings and sixpence, and a guinea is a pound and a shilling. This is how you write them down, sir, if you'd like me to show you."

He took his slate and wrote: Half-a-crown —   2s. 6d.

                              A guinea   £1 1s. 0d.

                                       £1 3s. 6d.

"And if you add them up," said the Old Monkey, "they come to one pound, three shillings and sixpence. Uncle says that the signs £ s. d. come from Latin words: he used to know them when he was at the University, but he's forgotten them now."

J. P. MARTIN (1879–1966) was born in Yorkshire into a family of Methodist ministers. He took up the family vocation, serving when young as a missionary to a community of South African diamond miners and then, during the First World War, as an Army chaplain in Palestine and Egypt, before returning to minister to parishes throughout the north of England. He died at eighty-six from a flu caught while bringing pots of honey to his parishioners in cold weather. Martin began telling Uncle stories to entertain his children, who later asked him to write them down so that they could read them to their own children; the stories were finally published as a book in 1964, when Martin was eighty-four. The jacket to the first edition of *Uncle* notes that "the inspiration for these stories seems to come from the industrial landscape that [Martin] knew as a child.... He still likes to take his family and friends on walks through industrial scenes. He also enjoys painting the wild and beautiful landscape where he lives. It is not enough to say he loves children; he is continually visited by them."

QUENTIN BLAKE is one of the most celebrated children's book illustrators working today, having illustrated more than three hundred books by such authors as Russell Hoban, Joan Aiken, and Roald Dahl. A prolific writer of books for children himself, Quentin Blake was appointed the first Children's Laureate of England in 1999.